The Witchlets of Witches Brew

The Witchlets of Witches Brew

Edain Duguay

Wyrdwood Publications
Canada

THIS BOOK IS PUBLISHED BY WYRDWOOD
PUBLICATIONS, OTTAWA, ON, CANADA

Visit us on the web: Wyrdwood Publications.com

Library and Archives Canada Cataloguing in Publication

Duguay, Edain, 1966-, author
The Witchlets of Witches Brew / Edain Duguay.

Short stories.
Issued in print and electronic formats.
ISBN 978-0-9879980-8-8 (pbk.)
ISBN 978-0-9879980-0-2 (ebook)

I. Title.
PS8607.U37623W57 2013   jC813'.6   C2013-907677-8
C2013-907678-6

First trade paperback (revised) edition,
copyright © March 2014

Dedication

I wish to dedicate these stories to my daughter, Melissa, who has always been my inspiration for life. Without you, I would not have been able to see the world through the eyes of a child, nor enjoy living that way.

You are a blessing to all that you meet, I love you.

Contents

Forward

The nine Witchlets of Witches Brew tales are centred round a year in the life of nine friends who are young Pagans and also Witches.

The friends: Holly, Birch, Ash, Willow, Ivy, Hazel, Rowan, Yew and Plum all live in the Village of Brew, commonly known by the name of 'Witches Brew'. You see, in the village of Brew, everyone is a Witch.

Now, these Witches are not like the ones you see in all the stories or at Halloween, who are little green ladies with pointy shoes, black pointy hats, black dresses and broomsticks.

No, these Witches are the real kind, they look and dress just like everyone else. They worship the land and the seasons; they celebrate all the wonders of life and nature during their eight special festivals each year.

The children all go to the local village school called, The Elementary School which is built in the shape of a Sun Wheel, with parts of the building facing each of the four directions North, East, South and West. Hence, the name is from the four Elements Earth, Air, Fire and Water.

Each of the Pagan celebrations for the seasons sees deep changes in each girl's life and every tale is relative to the yearly celebrations around which, it is set. Throughout these stories of change, the girls learn to become better people and find a way to appreciate life, family and nature more.

Holly the Hasty Witch

An Introduction to Holly

Everyone, including Holly's family, call her Hasty Holly. Holly was always rushing about, bumping into things, doing only half her house chores, not finishing her homework, always late and she never looks where she is going!

Holly is eleven years old and tall for her age, in fact she is the tallest in her class! She has long, dark brown hair, bright shiny blue eyes and a very slightly bent nose, which was the result of a ball game with her brother the previous summer.

Our tale begins on the afternoon before Yule. That is another name for the Winter Solstice, a time when we see very little of the sun. It is the shortest day and the sun's at its lowest point in the sky.

This is the time for celebrating the return of the sun and so with it, hopefully, the return of the growing season at Spring Equinox or Ostara. It is also the last chance to thank the Ancestors and to ask for the return of the sun. This is done by staying up through the longest night of the year, until the sun rises again and to look forward to the slow turn of the Wheel to springtime. The time that is spent, staying up to see the dawn, is called a vigil and the one at Yule is called the Yule Vigil.

The entire village of Brew attend the Yule Vigil every year and then have a huge party to celebrate at one of the village houses afterwards, this year it was Holly's family's turn to host the party.

Holly the Hasty Witch

Holly's family were preparing for the big celebration. Holly's mum had been baking all day while her dad was decorating the barn at the bottom of the garden, where the party was to be held after the Yule Vigil. Holly had been given the job of cutting out the paper banners in shapes of the Sun and Moon, symbols of the vigil, whilst her younger brother, Stone, was cutting out the Sun and Moon shapes in the new cookie dough that Mum had just rolled out for him. Holly sat cutting away; not really looking at what she was doing, just daydreaming. Daydreaming and enjoying the wonderful smell of the herb breads and the chocolate Crescent and Sun cookies, which were baking in the kitchen. She could almost taste the buttery, chocolaty taste of her Mum's yummy cookies.

Suddenly, without finishing her work and leaving everything spread out in the living room floor, Holly jumped up and ran upstairs to her room. She had a sudden urge to play with her pet rat Herby and work on her drawings for the picture book she was creating. Stroking Herby with one hand whilst drawing the round castle of her dreams, she was so lost in the effort that she didn't hear her Mum walk up behind her.

"Holly?" her Mum called sternly and made Holly jump. "You haven't finished the decorations, you said you would help get them done tonight." Holly's Mum was angry because Holly never finished anything and was always running off to do something 'more important'.

Holly picked up Herby and snuggled him "Sorry Mum, I will do it later." she gave her Mum her brightest smile "I promise."

"Make sure you do Holly, giving your word to do something is very important and you must do what you say you will. You should never give your word if you don't mean to keep it!" Holly's Mum turned and started to leave the room, then she suddenly stopped at the door and turned back. "Just think if nature decided not to keep her promise to us at every Yule and not bring back the sun. We would not be able to grow our food, never mind celebrate what she gives us, nor enjoy the turning of the seasonal wheel. There would be no celebration like our party tomorrow night to celebrate the returning of the Sun. Then where would we be?" Holly's Mum walked out of the room and went downstairs heading back to the kitchen.

Holly put Herby back on his favourite cushion, on the window ledge and could hear her Mum words float up the staircase as she was talking to Stone about his designs for the Jack-O-Lanterns and what he wanted for dinner that night.

Holly didn't think again about the paper decorations she was supposed to be doing, even though she had given her word to do it, instead she carried on drawing until her eyes became tired and drowsy. Giving in to the warmth of the sun shining through the window and her sleepiness, Holly fell sound asleep.

Holly awoke suddenly, she felt very hungry and wondered what her Mum had decided on for dinner, she jumped off her bed and ran down stairs to see when dinner would be. As usual Holly found everyone sat around the big Oak dinner table, whilst her Mum was bringing a big yellow crock pot over from the oven and placing it on the rattan mat in the middle of the table.

"I was about to call you, Holly." Her Mum smiled as she turned back towards the kitchen to fetch the bread, "Go and wash you hands quickly, so we can say the blessing."

Holly quickly washed her hands at the kitchen sink with her mum's homemade soap that smelt of Heather, she dried her hands, walked quickly back to the table and jumped into her seat. She was in her usual place between her Dad and Mum and opposite Stone. Holly was very hungry and couldn't wait to get into what looked like it could be one of her Mum's wonderful thick stews full of meat, potatoes and root vegetables from their large kitchen garden. These stews were usually served with her mum's yummy fresh baked bread and herb butter. Holly mouth was watering at the thought of her favourite meal. She held her plate up for her Mum to serve her, before her Mum had even sat down with the bread!

"Holly, wait," her Mum sat down, "you know the Blessing comes first." Mum reached out her hands to Holly and Stone and everyone joined hands and began the blessing. "Goddess, Mother to us all, we thank you for all our Blessings." Her Mum turned to Holly it was her turn to speak.

"Blessings for your seasons." Holly said with a big smile.

"Blessings for your produce." Dad said and looked at Stone.

"Blessings for your animals." Stone said proudly and looked at his Mum.

"Blessings for our family, your gifts of the Earth, Moon and Sun, so be it!" and with a flourish Mum pulled off the lid off the hotpot and reached out for Holly's plate to dish up the stew.

Holly was amazed, actually speechless. Her plate was full of a grey watery liquid with hardly any pieces in it, mostly little bits of potatoes and carrots. *Where was the thick, wonderfully tasty stew with big chunks of meat and vegetables?* She thought and looked up at her Mum and noticed she looked thinner in the face and tired, nervously Holly looked round at the rest of her family they were the same, they all had grey skin and all looked tired and unhappy.

Holly didn't understand. Even the bread on the table, which was usually thick and fluffy and freshly made each day by her Mum, was flatter and thinner and it looked stale and chewy. Holly looked around at the kitchen end of the dining room, *Where were Mums window plants?* She wondered. Her Mum loved different kinds of chillies and was always growing some on the window sill. Even the huge pot of Basil, which her Mum loved to smell and cook with, wasn't there!

"Mum, where are all your plants and what happened to all the nice vegetables and meat in your stew? Why does your bread look like Stone sat on it?" Holly's words rush out because she knew deep down that something was wrong, very wrong.

Stone giggled, put his hand over his smile and tried to look serious, Dad just looked at Holly obviously not knowing what to say, while Mum reached over and put her hand on Holly's forehead. "Are you alright, Holly? Do you feel unwell?" Mum asked with deep concern in her voice.

"I am fine, Mum. I don't understand, I could smell you cooking the pumpkin pie, cookies and bread earlier. Where are they? Where is the stew?" Holly looked at her Mum and then her Dad as if this was a joke and they were hiding the real food.

"Now Holly you know there has not been much food for this past year, you know nothing will grow in anyone's garden since the Sun decided not to come back last Yule. And you know very well that your Mum does her best with what we can find. Say you're sorry to your Mum!" Dad insisted angrily.

"But I don't know that." Holly squealed, she was frightened now. "I don't know anything about it. It's not true! Of course the Sun came back last Yule, we all stayed up to watch it as usual."

"Have you bashed your head rushing round upstairs again?" Mum came over to Holly and checked her pupils. "Are you sure your ok, hun?" Holly's Mum peered in for a closer look, "You should remember that the Sun never came back, you were there waiting for it with us and the rest of Brew."

"No, no, no... NNNOOOO. It did ....I saw it... it did, it did!" Holly jumped out of her chair and ran to the window looking for the Sun but of course it was always dark at dinner time in December! "It's not true, how can we live without the Sun? Doesn't it make everything grow, don't we need it to stay alive?" Holly could remember something from her science lessons at school about how every living thing would die without the Sun. "If the Mother Goddess didn't let the Sun keep its promise and come back at Yule, then we would all be dead, I know we learnt it in science." Holly said triumphantly as if that would make everything right again.

"Yes, Holly, you are right." Dad said with a sad note in his voice.

Holly looked pleased and hopeful that everything would be alright now.

Holly's Dad continued, "But that's what's happening. For some reason, and nobody knows why, the Mother Goddess decided not to return the Sun to us. Mother Nature broke her eternal promised and refused to let the Sun rise again. All the Scientists are baffled; they do not know why or how this happened, just that it has. How could you forget how hard we have tried to keep things growing by using electric lights? Don't you remember that all the gardens are now barren and dead? Everyone is getting ill because of it, too." Dad said while looking sadly at Mum, "We just have to keep trying and hope that tomorrow's celebration of what little we have, and our prayers for a better harvest next year are heard. Some people think that the Mother Goddess got fed up with humans wasting her bounty, ruining the planet by polluting even the very water, air and soil we need to live on. Maybe she decided to show us just what we would be without her. A lesson we have learnt the hard way, I think."

"But Dad, how can that be? All Witches worship the Earth and tread careful upon her, we recycle, we grow and eat organic, we only take and use what we need and we never kill for sport just for the family pot... so how can she not fulfil her word to us?" Holly asked with tears welling in her eyes.

"There are more people in the world than Witches, Holly. Some are wise and think like we do, others...well, others are always in a rush not caring what they do on the Earth, they waste energy, they do not care that they are poisoning the very planet they live on, just so they can make more money. These are the unwise people that must learn the hardest lesson. They have lost the old arts of living off the land and growing their own food. Once their shops ran out of food they had no idea of what to do and in the end they started to approach Witches for advice and lessons in nature's ways. It was hard for them, they had spent hundreds of years hating us, laughing at us and disliking us for being 'nature lovers' and 'tree huggers'. Well, now they have to learn our ways to live in harmony or they will lose everything including their lives." Dad explained.

"I still remember the Sun coming up last Yule, but it must be so if you say it is Dad. I know your word is good and I believe you. How will we celebrate tomorrow morning, if we have so little food? How will we feed everyone that is coming to the party?"

"We shall do it just like we always do, hon." Mum smiled at Holly as she sat back at the table and began eating her thin stew, "Our friends will bring whatever they have to share with everyone and no matter how much or how little there is we shall thank the Ancestors and the Mother Goddess for the bounty and perhaps she will uphold her promise to return the Sun to us this Yule." Mum said will a hopeful smile and passed the bread to Holly to tear a piece off and then pass it onto Dad.

The stew was thin but still tasty, Mum had done her best just as Dad had said.

"The stew is tasty Mum, I like it." Holly smiled at her Mum and she saw a smile appear on her Mums face immediately.

"I am glad you like it Holly, thank you." Mum squeezed Holly's hand knowing that the stew really wasn't that good.

Holly was quiet for the rest of the meal as she tried hard to understand what was happening. Soon the meagre meal was over, everyone helped Mum to clean up and wash the pots, it was Holly's and Stone's job to put away the dishes once Dad had washed and Mum had dried them. Soon the kitchen was tidy again and Mum started to get out her ingredients for Mulled Wine from their storage of homemade wine, it was traditional to have mulled wine through the vigil, as it kept everyone warm and cosy throughout the cold night. Another tradition was to have freshly baked cookies with the mulled wine but perhaps we would not get any of those this year Holly thought.

Holly decided that she would finish the job she had been given before dinner, the Sun and Moon decorations for the barn, she thought that it might cheer her Mum and Dad up.

Once Holly had finished cutting them out she gave them to her Dad, put on her boots and her winter coat and set off with him down to the Barn to help put them up. At the barn, Holly couldn't contain herself any longer and burst out, "Dad, why can't I remember the Sun not coming back? Why do I remember seeing it?"

"I don't know love, perhaps you dreamt you saw it come back because not having it made you so very sad?" Her Dad smiled kindly at her, making his face crinkle with smile lines.

He climbed up to the top of the ladder, which was lent against the stone inside wall of the barn, and he pinned up the first of the Sun decorations.

"Maybe...Dad, was I really sad? I don't remember." Holly asked in a quiet voice.

"Yes love, you were. Very sad, you know how much you love rushing around in the Sunshine and playing with your friends outside." He smiled gently at Holly trying to encourage her "I am sure the Mother Goddess will allow us the use of the Sun this year seeing as mankind has now gelled as one people to honour and take care of the earth and her creatures."

"I hope so Dad, I really do!" Holly looked at him hopefully. "I am off to help Mum, are you coming up to the Circle when you have finished the decorations?"

"Yes, love I will meet you all there soon, tell your Mum I will carry the chairs if she takes the blankets, mulled wine and whatever else she has been up too. Will you be a good girl and help her carry everything up the Goddess Mound to the Circle Holly?"

"Yes, I will." Holly called back as she was already heading back to the house, "Don't worry Dad, I will help her."

Two hours later the party food, what little there was, was ready in the barn for the party later and refreshments were packed and ready to be carried up the village mound. This rounded hump of a hill was known locally as the Goddess Mound as it looked like a big pregnant tummy. At the top there stood the huge stone circle of thirteen big stones, all of which had carvings of spirals on them. Some stones were tilting over and had lichen growing on the due to their age, but they all looked like they were stood watching over the village. This was the traditional place for all celebrations in Brew, from Festival Days to Handfastings, from Summer Plays to the Samhain Bonefire. Everyone from the village gathered there for the, much hoped for, rise of the Sun at the Winter Solstice. Afterwards all the villages will attend the party on that year's host's land, this year it was Holly's parent's honour.

Holly shoulder was aching from carry the flasks of mulled wine but finally she made it to the top of the Goddess Mound and found that most of the village was already there. People were sat on chairs or blankets or stood around talking to their friends in groups. Holly spotted her friends Ivy and Yew and waved to them.

Holly's Mum found a nice spot near the Baker, his wife and their sons, Oak and Thorn, who were already asleep at their feet but they were very little, Oak was four and Thorn was only two. Little ones are not expected to stay awake all night, their parents will wake them when (if) the sun begins to show.

Holly's Mum just got the rugs laid out with the mulled wine, blankets and others things arranged on it when Holly's Dad arrived with the chairs. He opened them up and everyone sat down and started to relax now that everything was done for the party.

"Mum...?" asked Holly

"Yes, Holly?"

"What happens if the Sun doesn't return again this year?" Holly looked worried.

"Well, we shall cope somehow just like we have for the last year." Mum tried to look brave but Holly could see the worry in her eyes.

"That is a very good question, Holly." Dad said "I was just thinking the same, I think I will go over and talk to the Elders to see what the plans are for the next year." He got up and walked over to a group of men and women who are the village Elders. The Elders look after the village, made the laws and the important decisions about the land, crops and celebrations. They are very wise and much respected by everyone.

"Do you remember anything about this last year, Holly?" Mum asked with a worried frown.

"I remember the whole year, I just don't remember it being dark." Holly said.

Perhaps tomorrow we should go as see Elder Heather, perhaps she can help with her herbs, maybe she can bring the memory of the Sun not returning back to you. What do you think? I could mention it to her later." Mum reached over and gave Holly a hug.

"I think that might be a good idea, Mum." Holly looked hopeful and was pleased to be going to see Elder Heather. Holly loved Elder Heather and her busy house; it was full of plants, drying herbs, potions, lotions, jars full of herbs and roots. She also had many cats all of which loved children and wanted to be fussed a lot. Elder Heather is also one of the teachers at school; she gave lessons on Herbology and she was a kind, wise lady and important Elder too. Holly knew she would be able to help her.

As the night drew in, the air was starting to get chilly and although some warmth was given out by everyone from the village in the same area, the winter's cold wind was starting to seep through Holly's coat and make her shiver. Mum spotted the shivers and wrapped Holly in a thick wool blanket with a smile and a hug.

Holly spotted her friends nearby and decided to go and chat with them for a while, hoping to pass a couple of hours until sunrise.

"Mum, I am off to see Ivy & Yew...they're just over there." Holly pointed to a group of children sat around the main stone of the circle.

"Ok hun, but if you get cold again come back for some mulled wine." Mum snuggled Stone up on her knee and wrapped a blanket around them both.

On Festival Day Celebrations, Holly was allowed small drinks of wine, mead or mulled wine and she loved them all, and so she was looking forward to feeling colder later.

She walked around several people and smiled at Birch the Firekeeper, a big kind man with a wonderful long beard, he was setting up the Yule fire to keep everyone warm during the ritual. Holly made her way through the gathered people towards her friends and sat down next to Ivy. Ivy is also tall and very thin even though she could out eat everyone. Holly loved her friend dearly; she was fun but could be very stubborn too. Ivy had long dark hair and brilliant green eyes, which she turned on Holly as she sat down.

"Hi Holly, getting cold isn't it?" Ivy smiled, happy to see her friend.

Holly snuggled up next to Ivy "Yup it is, where are the others?" Holly looked round but with so many people it was hard to spot all her friends.

"Yew has just gone to get a blanket from her Grandma, Willow and Rowan went to get some food from Rowan's Mum. I haven't seen the others yet though." Explained Ivy.

"Ah...they'll be here somewhere...do you think the Sun will come back this year?" Holly looked into Ivy's eyes.

"Oh yes, it will... I am convinced. The Goddess is just trying to teach man a lesson, that's what my Dad says" Ivy was totally confident.

"I wish I believed that," said Holly, "but I can't believed it has been gone."

"What do you mean you can't believe it, you have spent this last year without it just as we have? How can you not believe it?" Ivy looked shocked.

"For some reason, I can't remember it being dark for the last year, I remember the Sun shining, I remember us all playing down at the river and in the old woods with bright sunshine and I remember flowers growing and gardens full of vegetables everywhere around the village. I don't remember any dark!" Holly was glad to have said it all and got it out of her mind.

"Oh." Ivy frowned. "Are you ill? Have you lost your memory?" Ivy looked worried for her friend.

"No, I remember everything from Oak the younger's fall in the river to last Mid Summer's Picnic when we danced in Circle of Stones as flowers. Only it all had Sunshine." Holly explained.

"Well, that was definitely last year! Weird though that you had Sun but we didn't, huh?" Ivy said thoughtfully. "Have you spoken to Elder Heather about this? She might be able to help."

Yew arrived with her blanket and sat down next to Ivy "Hi Holly. Elder Heather could help with what? What did I miss?" Yew smiled impishly.

Yew was very clever and yet always got bored quickly. She was small with short spiky blond hair and horn rimmed glasses, she snuggled deeper into the double thickness of her Grandmas multi-coloured knitted blanket.

"Holly can't remember that this entire year has been dark." Ivy sounded astounded.

"What? Since when? Are ya nuts?" Yew laughed.

"Thanks. No, I am not nuts. I just don't get it, I can remember everything except the sun being gone. Well no, that's wrong, actually I remember the Sun and we all had nice gardens and food like before but everyone else says the year has been totally dark." Holly looked from Ivy to Yew and back again, "Any ideas why I can't remember...apart from me being nuts, that is." Holly said.

"Hmm...that's a tricky one. I now see why Elder Heather might help or perhaps Elder Daisy as she is the Mistress of Women's Mysteries or how about Elder Furze perhaps could help, him being the Master of the Male Mysteries...it being about the sun and all. Maybe they would have some reason for it." Yew suggested, "But I wouldn't go and see them now as all the Elders are talking to the villagers over by the High Stone, I think I saw your Dad with them too, looks like it is an in depth conversation. I guess it will be about how the village will survive without the Sun for another year."

"Oh, don't say that." Cried Ivy, "I just know it will come back, there is no way we can last another year."

"Now that is a scary thought." Holly said and they all huddled closer together.

Birch had by now got a roaring Yule fire going in the firepit in the centre of the circle, people were starting to huddled around it, some had started drumming and others were singing the traditional song 'Calling of the Sun', asking it to come back to warm her children. Holly had always loved this song and so was happy to just sit and listen to it. Soon the words of the song and the rhythmical pounding of the drums relaxed Holly and made her feel that everything would be ok. The call of the song and drums would be heard by the Sun and he would return to us once again and Nature would fulfil her promise to her children.

The evening hours moved into the mornings early hours. Holly had spent much time with her friends talking about her inability to remember the darkness of the past year but no one could give her any answers and they all agreed that Elder Heather, Elder Daisy and Elder Furze should be consulted tomorrow when hopefully the Sun was back. As time wore on, Holly could feel the nervous energy of the people all singing, dancing and playing drums for hours to try to persuade the Sun to rise again.

With so many people around the fire all huddled together no one seemed to notice the cold of the winter's night. Hot drinks were passed around in an assortment of containers from carved horn mugs to pottery cups, everyone sharing and everyone focusing on the same thing: the Sun.

Slowly Holly and her friends started to return to their families as tiredness crept into their bones. Holly headed back to her family's area to find Mum and Dad stood talking to Rowan's parents and Stone was fast asleep on the rugs under several blankets. Holly decided that this would be the warmest place to wait until it was time so she cuddled up to her young brother in his warm blanket cave.

Holly was warm and cosy within the blankets and soon found herself drifting off into a light sleep, she seemed to be between sleep and awake as she was too heavy to move her arms or legs but she could hear the village people talking, drumming and singing in the background. The time passed slowly but it was cosy and warm so Holly didn't mind.

Holly's mind drifted back to the summer holidays when she played in the woods and fields with her friends, she was certain the sun was there, she had no memory of the darkness. Had Nature broken her word and not keep her promise to her children to bring back the Sun last Yule or had everyone been hypnotized or are they playing a joke on her and everything is normal but how then do you explain the lack of flowers, vegetable and plants everywhere? Holly was afraid, afraid of why she couldn't remember if it was real and if it was real, what it would mean for everyone?

How can we all live without the Sun?

Holly half dozed for a while and had strange disjointed dreams, which made no sense to her. She cuddled up to Stone and thought that no matter what is happening with the Sun she knew that the villagers would all stick together and do the best they could to get through it.

Holly could hear murmurs of excitement and it roused her from her snooze, the noise was many people excitedly talking at once. Suddenly, Mum's voice could be heard through the noise "Wake up, Holly. Wake up, Stone. Wake up. Come and see this..." Mum called urgently.

Holly and Stone sprang up out of the covers, they were suddenly and totally awake. "What is it? What's wrong?" Holly asked whilst looking around for a disaster or something else that could have made her Mum so excited. Everything looked normal. Everyone was looking to the sky and they were all talking excitedly. Holly turned to look in the same direction but could see nothing unusual just the night sky.

"Look, I think the sky is getting lighter, can you see it?" Mum asked.

Holly watched the sky for a while as her eyes readjusted slowly from being asleep. "Not sure Mum, not sure I see any difference." Holly said and rubbed her eyes.

Everyone was standing now and looking to the East to where the Sun should come up over the horizon.

"Yes, see it is getting lighter, the Sun is returning!" Mum cried out with joy.

Instantly everyone saw the same thing and there was a sudden burst of cheering, clapping and shouting. People were dancing, singing and drumming to encourage the Sun more, joy and happiness overflowed from everyone as Nature kept her promise to her children and the sky quickly started to lighten, announcing the return of the Sun.

The celebration got louder as everyone released they had be tense awaiting this moment. It was hard to hear each other speak but no one minded, as the Sun eventually peeped over the horizon and shone its wonderful warm light on all. Everyone cheered and clapped as the Elders lead a prayer of thanks and celebration for the return of the Sun and the eternal promise kept.

Holly hugged her Mum fiercely and was jumping up and down "It's back, the Sun is back...no more darkness." Holly grabbed her brother and danced around with him. "The promise has been kept."

"You're mad." Stone said, while giggling.

Holly continued to dance wildly and she grabbed her Dad and hugged him, "The Sun is back Dad, it's back." Holly shouted "Now we can have proper meat and vegetable stew." Holly laughed.

"Of course it's back. Nature always keeps her promises." Dad shouted back. "What's that about meat and vegetable stew? You hungry?" He asked.

"Yes, I am hungry, very hungry for big fat juicy vegetables" Holly was overjoyed that the Sun had returned. She looked at the new dawn; it was all pinks and soft yellows as the Sun gathered its strength for the Winter Solstice Day.

"I am glad the Sun came back, I do not want to have another year without it." Holly said with relief and hugged her Dad again.

Dad hugged Holly back, "What do you mean, Holly?" Dad knelt down in front of Holly and looked up into her eyes, "What do you mean another year without it?" Dad smiled but looked worried.

"You know, Dad." Holly beamed. "We had to live last year without the Sun and all the gardens died and I missed the vegetables in Mum's stew." She smiled as the words tumbled out quickly and she looked at her Dad as if he was playing with her.

"Of course the Sun returned last year Holly, it is a cycle that can not be stopped, that is half of what we celebrate at Yule, are you alright?" Dad looked concerned and called Mum over.

"Holly thought that the Sun wouldn't come back." Dad explained to Mum.

"Not....just not come back, but we had a year of dark because it didn't come back last year, you remember, Dad. I couldn't remember and you all told me about it at dinner." Holly looked from her Mum to her Dad. "And all the plants died and there was hardly any food for dinner."

"Oh Holly, you must have been dreaming. The Sun came back last year, Nature will always keep her promises to bring the Sun and the Seasons back for her children." Mum hugged Holly, "Are you sure you are ok?" She kissed Holly's forehead.

"Yes, I am fine... it might have been a dream I suppose, I could remember the Sun last year and everyone kept telling me it was dark, it just didn't make sense." Holly said in a relieved voice, happy to have things back to normal.

"Well, at least you now understand the importance of the Sun returning to us. Would you help me take the blankets and things down the Mound, back to the house, folks will be moving off the mound and towards our barn very soon." Mum asked.

"Sure, I'll help. Come on Stone help me fold this blanket up." Holly turned and started folding the blanket.

The villagers around them were starting to gather their things and pack them away, making their way back to Holly's family barn for food and the Yule party. Holly took one last look at the now totally risen Sun, a beautiful orange golden globe just on the horizon and sighed, she felt a lightness of heart that no other Sunrise had ever given her, she had been very frightened deep inside and was truly thankful that Nature had kept her promise.

Holly and her family arrived at their barn just ahead of the villagers and began uncovering the food, setting the wine and mead to mull over a low heat on the camping stoves. Dad started to heat up the thick delicious stews and bean mixtures, there were rolls, hot creamy cheesy soups, there were large pieces of ham, beef and pork being sliced, roasted vegetables. Still more trays of mouth watering food was being brought in by the villagers, everyone had brought something to share in both food and drink and within ten minutes the barn was full of celebrating people and tables heavy with wondrous food.

The local band 'Moon Scape' had started playing a jig at the end of the barn and folks were already dancing, eating, drinking and laughing. Holly sat with Rowan and Ivy and explained what she could only describe as her dream of the Dark Year.

"I am so happy it was just a dream. It would be terrible if that really happened." Said Ivy as she tucked into her bowl full of creamy cheesy soup.

"Wow, what a dream." Rowan said while munching on a big beef roll, "That soup looks good, I'm off to get some." Rowan went off to help herself. Rowan was small and slim, yet would eat everything and anything presented to her. She had short naturally curly brown hair and big brown eyes and had vanished into the crowd around the food tables in seconds.

"Odd though, I wonder what it all means." Ivy pondered, "I think you should talk to Elder Daisy she may know about women's dreams seeing as she is the Mistress of Women's Mysteries."

Holly laughed, "You know, Yew suggested that I talked to her in my dream."

"Well, great minds think alike." Ivy giggled, "Where is Yew?"

"She is getting her Grandma some food, I saw her at the tables a little while ago." Replied Holly. "I think I will talk to Elder Daisy and see what she thinks to it all, I'm glad it was just a dream but it seemed so real at the time. I can remember everything that happened, even the smell of Mum sad little stew."

"Hmm...it's very interesting, talk to Elder Daisy tonight so you can tell me what she thinks." Said Ivy as she put down her soup bowl and sipped her drink.

"I think I will Ivy, but first I am off to get some food...this dreaming makes you hungry. See you later." Holly laughed and smiled goodbye to Ivy, she made her way to her Mum at the food tables.

"How is it going, Mum?"

"Very well actually, I love hosting parties and seeing everyone having fun, your decorations look great hon." Mum said as she removed an empty plate of egg sandwiches from the table and replaced it with a full one.

Holly looked round the hall, she had to agree her decorations did look good and she was proud of them. Holly picked up a china plate and began to help herself to some food, it was difficult to choose what to have as it all looked so tasty. She took some raw veggies and dip which was her favourite, then a couple of sandwiches and a small bowl of the creamy cheesy soup too and went to sit next to her Dad who was keeping an eye on the stews and other foods that were warming on the camp stoves.

"Are you doing ok, Holly?" Dad asked and spooned some thick stew into his mouth with a grin.

"Yep, I am great Dad, very happy it was a dream. I have decided to ask Elder Daisy what she thinks of it." Holly said as she was finishing her plate of food.

"Now that is a good idea, when I see her I'll tell her you're looking for her, shall I?" asked Dad.

"That would be great Dad, thanks. Hmm...this soup is very good." Said Holly.

"I have not had any yet, I just can't get past ya Mum's stew, it is so good." Dad laughed.

"Oh that sounds good, can I have some too please?" As she swallowed the last of her cheesy soup.

Dad spooned out a small bowl of hot stew and put a garlic buttered roll with it. "Here you go love." Dad handed the steaming bowl to Holly, "Isn't that Elder Daisy over there talking to Yew's Grandma?" Dad pointed to the far side of the barn, where two grey haired ladies we chatting.

"Thanks, Dad." Holly took the stew and roll then looked across the barn and saw that it was Elder Daisy and the chair on the other side of her was empty. "I shall go and see what she say's, tell you about it later." Holly was off across the barn with her soup before her dad could say anything.

Elder Daisy was small and curvy with one of those faces that never stops smiling, she always made everyone feel happy and relaxed and so many came to her for advice, she also had a very gentle and soft voice that help others to be calm around her. She had shoulder length thick hair which was wavy and totally silver. Elder Daisy was dressed in jeans, boots, shirt and big woolly multi-coloured cardigan that looked like it was the work of Yew's Grandma, a self-confessed knit-wit.

Holly smiled at both Elder Daisy and at Yew's Grandma, Elder Flower, sat down next to Elder Daisy and started eating her stew. It was wonderful, just how she remembered her Mum's stew should taste, not that horrid watery thin stuff of her dream. The freshly made roll with homemade garlic butter mixed with the stew so well and Holly was enjoying them both so much that she missed what Elder Daisy said to her.

"I am sorry Elder Daisy, what did you say?" Asked Holly.

"I said you look like you are enjoying that stew, is it your Mum's famous meat and veggie stew?" She asked smiling.

"Oh yes, and it is so good." Holly wiped the last piece of bread around the empty bowl. "But sadly it's gone now, well gone until the next time." Holly laughed.

"That's a wise thing to say." Laughed Elder Daisy. "Now tell me what is troubling you, Holly?"

"How did you know something was bothering me?" Holly was amazed.

"Ah...well, that is my job you see, to spot when something is wrong and try to work out what's going on. I can see in your eyes that you are worried about something, what is it that brings you worry, my dear?"

Holly told Elder Daisy all about her dream of the dark year and that she couldn't remember the dark in her dream although everyone else knew about it. She told her about how all the plants had died and food was getting hard to find and how everyone looked ill. She told her how she had not realised how much she loved the Sun until she had awoken from the dream and saw the dawn of the Winter Solstice Sun. All the information tumbled out of Holly mouth in one big rush. Holly finally sat there quiet having emptied her heart to Elder Daisy.

"Hmm...what an interesting time you've been having, Holly." Elder Daisy put her arm around Holly and gave her a reassuring hug, "But was it a dream?"

"What do you mean?" Holly asked, "What else could it be?"

"Well it could be a number of things, it could be a dream yes, but it could also be a message of some sort...or a premonition but lets hope it wasn't. Or it could have been a lesson of some kind. What do you feel it was, deep down inside you?" Elder Daisy said.

"I'm not sure. At first I thought it was a dream but then it didn't feel like a dream, I don't know how to explain that but it just didn't." Holly looked for understanding from Elder Daisy and saw it in her face.

"Ok, how about a message or premonition?"

"Hmm...not so much a message and I don't think it was a premonition as it was set now and not in the future, if that makes sense?" Replied Holly.

"Perfect sense, Holly. If something makes sense to you and feels right for you, then it is right for you. So do you think it could be a lesson of some kind?" Elder Daisy said while sipping her mulled wine.

"Maybe, but I do not understand it if it was a lesson. What would a dark year be teaching me or would the lack of memory of the Dark Year be the lesson or...I don't know." Holly sighed.

"Don't worry Holly, let's think about it for a moment and see what we can come up with shall we?"

"Ok." replied Holly.

They both sat in silence for a while watching the villagers gather around the large Yule tree, the smaller children were getting last minute instructions from their parents about handing out the Yule presents. You see, in the village of Brew everyone's name is put into a hat at Samhain in October, each person picks out a name and that is the person they are to make one present for. This way, no matter what, every person in the village gets a gift at Yule. The gift is presented to them by the smallest members of the community, some with a little help from their parents.

Finally, Elder Daisy turned to Holly and said, "I think I have it." She smiled, "As you know, some lesson can be difficult to take in, as a person may believe that they are doing fine when they are not."

"Yes, I understand what you mean. What do you think my lesson is Elder Daisy?" Holly held her breath.

"I think your lesson from this is to follow the example of Mother Nature and always keep your promises." Elder Daisy smiled brightly at Holly "You are known as Hasty Holly because you rush around, not finishing anything nor keeping your promises, making those around you angry or sad. I think you were shown what it would be like if Nature didn't keep her promise to all her children. What do you think?"

Holly thought about this for several minutes before answering, "I think you are right Elder Daisy, I think that is exactly what this is about and the lesson for me. I understand now and I agree, I do leave things half done and sometimes I forget the promises I have made." Holly shyly smiled at Elder Daisy.

"I am glad you understand your lesson Holly, make sure you learn from it too."

"Oh I will, from now on my promises will mean something to everyone including me. I shall finish what I have started and I shall in future make my word mean something." Holly gave Elder Daisy a very big hug, "Thank you for helping me see the lesson."

"You are very welcome Holly, thank you for bringing this to me." Elder Daisy hugged back.

Holly stood, picked up her bowl and told Elder Daisy she would see her later. She had decided to go and tell her parents and her friends straight away about her lesson and what she had learnt.

Elder Daisy watched Holly walk back towards the crowd around the food and the Yule Tree, knowing that this lesson had been learnt and she was glad for it.

Birch the Selfish Witch

An Introduction to Birch

For many years, each child of Brew has been named after various items within Nature and Birch is no exception.

Named after the Birch tree, which is one of the first trees to grow on bare soil and it has come to symbolize fertility, healing and rebirth. The tree itself was used for almost everything from canoes to producing sugar and represents that which is needed for everyday living. It is also known for its protective healing abilities and is used to drive out evil spirits and as protection from the fairy folk.

Birch is eleven years old with very short brown hair and brown eyes. She is slightly smaller than the average height of her friends and has a medium build.

Unfortunately, Birch is a selfish and sad girl. She never used to be, but then her life changed drastically four years ago and although her mum and Birch got through the hard times together, life at home changed yet again and Birch just didn't feel like she fitted in anymore.

Our tale begins at the end of January, just before the Imbolc celebration otherwise known as Seeding Day. This is a time when seeds are planted and nurtured to flourish throughout the coming year and a time of the returning light when new paths should be attempted in life.

Birch the Selfish Witch

Birch looked at the calendar and noticed it was only one week until Imbolc and the due date of 'it'.

She sighed deeply.

At eleven years old, she thought she was too old to have a baby brother or sister. Whatever it was, it would smell, make lots of noise and everyone would love it and pamper it. Even worse they would all make silly cooing noises over it. She shuddered at the thought. She also knew, without a doubt, that she would be invisible in one week's time, as soon as 'it' arrived.

Birch leant her head against the cold glass of her bedroom window, her breath making steam clouds on the pane. She looked out over the back garden towards the old forest and the Goddess Mound in the distance. On the mound she could see the villager's ritual space, the thirteen stones set in a ring each of them pointing upwards into the twilight sky like grey fingers reaching for the stars.

With a deep breath, and a sad face, she turned from the window looking back into her bedroom, her eyes scanned the posters of pop stars and horses that covered every inch of her bedroom walls. Sometimes she wished she could have her own horse and ride away on it or be someone famous and travel the world with millions of fans adoring her.

The worse part was that when her Dad was alive, he and Mum were so happy to have Birch, they called her their little miracle. They were never able to have more children, although Mum had got pregnant twice more, but she had lost them very early in the pregnancies. Then suddenly Birch's Dad had died in a car accident and it was just Birch and her Mum against the world.

They had done everything together, they'd shopped, cooked, gone on holidays and played together. They even saw each other everyday as her mum worked at the village school where Birch attended. Whenever both of them had a problem they would always sit at the kitchen table eating chocolate and devising a plan of attack to solve the problem together. They were inseparable.

That was until her mum had met Rock, she had met him while out at the village shops. Before long Rock and her mum were Handfasted and then suddenly Birch wasn't so special anymore and stopped being spoilt by her Mum. Rock had once told her Mum that she spoilt Birch too much and Birch knew he was right, but she had rather liked it. Apart from this, Rock and Birch had become good friends and she was happy that her Mum was happy.

Until now.

Until they announced that another miracle had happened and the Gods had blessed them with another child. Now, months later, the child was due to arrival in one week's time and was known, at least to Birch, as 'it'.

Birch could hear Rock arriving home from work for the evening. He was a butcher by trade and worked in the village butcher's shop. She knew she should be helping her mum with dinner as her mum had gotten so big with 'it' that she looked like an alien and it was easy for Birch to think of the baby as an alien. An alien that was making her mum huge, uncomfortable and would take over their lives.

Birch hated the thought of the new baby and made sure she avoided all conversations about it. Why should she pretend to look forward to it? Wasn't she taught that if she had nothing nice to say then to say nothing at all?

Birch spotted an empty cup on her dresser, bent to pick it up, brushed her hand through her very short brown hair so it stuck up just how she liked it and ran downstairs to help her Mum. Guilt forcing her to move, even if she did so with bad grace.

"Hey, slow down!" Rock said as he walked past the bottom of the stairs.

"Sorry." Birch grinned, "I didn't see you."

"Obviously, we're having pizza for dinner, I don't suppose you want any?" He said holding the box high up in the air with a big smile on his face.

"Cool." Birch tried to reach up but was not tall enough, still she tried again and failed. She continued to jump up at the box as she followed him into the kitchen laughing.

"There you are. I wondered where you had got to, Birch." Her Mum said to her from her seat at the dinner table, she turned her head for the 'welcome home' kiss from Rock. "How was your day, love?" She said to him.

"Pretty good as usual, how about you?" He gently placed his hand on her huge tummy and smiled as the baby kicked.

Birch could see her Mum's tummy ripple from where she sat. It made her shudder, how horrible to have a big thing inside you wriggling about. She thought of an octopus and had to look away quickly before her mum saw the horror on her face.

"I finished sorting the baby's clothes today, we're ready for the little one as soon as the baby decides to make an appearance." Mum said to Rock as she also placed her hand on her tummy.

"I hope you didn't work too hard, you need your rest."

Birch looked down at her empty plate, hoping food would come soon. She hated it when they spoke about the baby, what about her? No one asked if she'd had a good day at school or what she had been doing today.

Finally, Rock opened the pizza box and told her to dig in. He had bought Birch's favourite type home, a 'Meat Supreme', it was covered with pepperoni, ham and mushrooms. The pizza still didn't cheer her up though, she always felt left out when they talked about the baby and these days it was all they talked about. Birch took two pieces and sat quietly eating them while her Mum and Rock talked about whether the baby would arrive by the due date, after or even early. Both off them sounded excited, which made Birch even more miserable.

As soon as dinner was over, Birch washed the plates and cups for her Mum and disappeared off to her room claiming she had a lot of homework to do. It was true, she did, but it was not as urgent as she had claimed. She just couldn't spend all night hearing them talk about 'it'.

Birch switched on her computer and found she had a message from her best friend Hazel. Although, they saw each other everyday at school, Hazel and Birch always spent some of the night messaging each other. Hazel was such a fun friend, always interested in doing what she shouldn't and often getting in trouble. Birch didn't mind she loved all the attention the two of them got whenever they were caught doing something bad.

Birch scanned through the message. Everyone was making plans for the Imbolc celebration at the Stones and Birch and her friends were getting their new dresses ready for the maiden procession. Birch had been sewing her dress by hand as her Mum hadn't remembered to do it. This had made Birch very angry, she knew her Mum could usually be found sitting on the sofa most of the day reading, so she knew she had plenty of time to sew the dress for her if she had wanted to. In her last email to Hazel, Birch had, yet again, complained about the new baby, telling Hazel that her Mum doesn't have time for her now. How much worse would it be when it arrives? She asked. She wished they were not having a baby and that she could still be her Mum's little miracle.

Over the next few days, Birch finished sewing her own dress for the Imbolc procession and went to practice the ritual, with the other children of the village, at Elder Daisy's house. Elder Daisy, the Mistress of Women's Mysteries, looked like the most lovable Grandmother you could imagine. She was small and round, with one of those faces that never stops smiling, she always made everyone feel happy and relaxed and, because of this, many came to her for advice. She also had a very gentle and soft voice that helped others to be calm around her. She had shoulder length thick hair, which was wavy and completely silver. Birch thought it floated around her head as if she was underwater.

Elder Daisy was always very kind to the children, making them feel special and loved. Secretly, Birch wished she could live with her, but she had never told anyone this. At least she asked Birch what she'd been doing and how school was every time she saw her. Birch felt wanted and important around Elder Daisy.

It was towards the end of the ritual practice when Birch felt reluctant to go home, she wished she could stay in Elder Daisy's lovely little cottage forever and sighed deeply as she slowly pulled on her winter boots while the other children left. Hazel had already been picked up by her elder brother, Drake, who had offered to take Birch home, but she'd said no claiming she wanted to talk to Elder Daisy.

Birch sat back down by the fire in the living room to tie her laces and watched Elder Daisy see the rest of the children out.

She was soon back and settling herself in her big soft chair, offering Birch more hot chocolate.

"You seem like you could use this today and I guess you're not in a hurry." She said.

"Thank you." Birch reached out for the mug and snuggled back into the chair holding the warm cup against her tummy looking into the flames of the fire.

"How is your Mum?" Elder daisy asked.

"Big."

"It must be nearly time for the baby."

"Hmmm." Birch took a sip of the hot chocolate and continued to look into the flames, hoping Elder Daisy would change the subject.

"Tell me dear, what's troubling you?"

"Nothing." Birch hunched down into the chair more.

"Obviously something is, do you want to talk about it?" Elder Daisy reached over and placed her warm hand on top of Birch's, "I may be able to help." She said.

Birch looked Elder Daisy's kind face and decided not to tell her how she felt about the baby. She knew no one would understand and just think her mean. She quickly changed the subject, returning it to the upcoming celebration of Imbolc and finished her hot chocolate before miserably making her way back home in the cold night air.

Fleur, Birch's mum, was sat on the sofa as usual, in her dressing gown and PJ's, with her feet up. She was sat reading a book when Birch arrived home from the practice.

"Everything alright, dear?" Fleur said as Birch took off her coat and hung it on a peg near the front door.

"Hmmm..."

"Rock should be back soon, he just popped next door. Apparently, they've found some baby stuff in their attic and they want us to have it. Isn't that kind of them?" Mum smiled up at Birch.

"Uh huh..." Birch said as she headed towards the stairs as quickly as she could.

"Birch? Come and sit with me for a moment, please."

Birch sighed quietly to herself and returned to the living room where she stood impatiently at the end of the sofa by her mum's feet.

"Sit down a moment, love."

"I have homework to do." Birch said without moving.

"This won't take long. Please." Mum said as she slowly managed to sit up on the sofa, placing her book on the side table next to the lamp.

Birch threw herself down on a nearby chair, not want to be there at all. She absentmindedly played with the charm bracelet on her wrist.

"You seem to be unhappy lately. What's bothering you, love?" Fleur asked.

"Nothing." Birch replied without looking up.

"Come on, I know something is the matter. Talking about whatever it is will help. You know what they say: 'a problem shared is a problem halved'." Fleur smiled encouragingly.

"I don't care what 'they' say. There's nothing wrong." Birch glared at her mum.

"Birch, don't get angry with me, love. I just want to help." Fleur reached out her hand to touch Birch's knee.

"Help me?" Birch fumed and jumped up, she stood looking down at her mum, "How can you help me when you don't even know I'm alive!" She shouted.

"Of course, I know you're alive. Don't be silly, love. Whatever is the matter?"

Birch watched her Mum struggle to the edge of the sofa and try to stand up, the bulk of the baby making her movements difficult.

"No, you don't. You don't care about me anymore now that...that it's coming." Birch gestured towards Fleur's pregnant tummy, "All you care about is the stupid baby!" Birch burst into tears and ran from the room. She rushed up the stairs to her bedroom and slammed the door behind her. Sobbing, she threw herself on her bed and cried into her pillow.

She could hear her mum calling her from downstairs but refused to answer her and put her pillow over her head to block out the sound of her mum's voice.

Suddenly a high-pitched screech pierced through Birch's sobs and she heard a very loud noise like the chimney falling off the roof. She sat upright on her bed listening, tears still wet on her face. There was no sound, nothing further to help her work out what she'd heard, perhaps it had been an owl she thought. She listened hard again for a few moments and walked quietly to her door and listened there. What if someone had broken in? She started to feel nervous as she listened harder.

Nothing. Not a squeak of a floorboard.

Quietly, Birch opened her door and peeked out. Everything appeared normal and as it should be. Slowly she walked along the corridor towards the stairs starting to think she had been hearing things. At the top of the stairs, she froze unable to believe her eyes.

At the bottom of the stairs was a jumbled pile of clothing, at least it looked like one at first glance. Instantly, Birch realized that it wasn't a pile of clothing but her mum's bathrobe tangled up and her mum was laid in a very strange position. More horrifying was the fact that her mum was not moving.

Birch rushed down the stairs, almost falling herself in her rush to get to her mum.

"Mum?" She managed to climb over her mum's inert body to see her face. She looked like she was asleep. "Mum? MUM?" Birch tried to gently shake her arm hoping to wake her up but nothing worked. She was paralysed with fear that her mum was dead and couldn't move to get help.

"Hello?" Came a familiar voice.

"Her...here." Birch's voice croaked out feebly.

"By the Gods! What happened?" Rock dropped the box he was carrying and rushed over to the foot of the stairs, he took one look at Fleur and grabbed his phone from his pocket and dialled for an ambulance.

The next two hours were a blur of faces and white walls for Birch as her mother was taken into hospital and then into emergency surgery. Rock had said that she was bleeding inside from the fall and that both her life and that of the baby's were in danger. He had explained all this while they sat waiting in the family room. He held Birch close to him now, both of them were stunned and shocked that everything had changed so quickly and taken such a dangerous turn.

All Birch could think of was that if she hadn't fallen out with her mum and ran upstairs, her mum would not have followed her and fallen down the stairs. The thought of 'what if I've killed mum and the baby?' kept going round her head like a stuck song, making her feel more and more panicked.

"It's all my fault." She whispered to herself, still wrapped in Rocks arms. "My fault."

"Did you say something?" He asked pulling her away to see her face.

"It's all my fault."

"What is?"

"That mum and the baby are dying. It's all my fault." She said as she collapsed back into his arms and sobbed.

Rock stroked her hair away from her forehead. "Of course it isn't. It was an accident and they are not going to die." He sounded very determined.

"It is. I shouted at her and ran to my room. If I hadn't she wouldn't have followed me and fallen down the stairs. She will die because of me!" Birch's voice rose in pitch as the panic set in.

Rock pulled her away from him again. "Look at me." He placed his hand under her chin and lifted her face. "I said look at me, Birch."

Reluctantly she looked up at him.

"Now listen to me. Your mum and the baby are not going to die. They are both in a little trouble right now and that is why they are doing an emergency caesarean but neither of them will die. Do you hear me?"

Birch nodded miserably.

"And none of this is your fault. She could have easily just been going to the bathroom and fell down the stairs. No one is to blame, it was just an accident. Understand?"

Birch nodded.

Rock pulled her against him again. "Everything will be okay, I promise." He said as he gently rocked her and went back to staring at the door of the hospital's family room, waiting for news.

Although some of the immediate panic had drained away, Birch still wasn't totally convinced that both her mum and the baby would be okay. The more she thought about them both, the more she felt guilty for ever wishing that the baby didn't exist.

At last, after what seemed like hours, the door opened and in walked a doctor dressed in scrubs.

"Mr. Ackart?" He said.

Rock stood quickly, "Yes?"

"You wife and child are recovering. Both are well considering and congratulations you are the father of a beautiful baby girl." The doctor smiled.

"Oh...thank you. They're both alright?" Rock said, trying to take in the good news.

"Yes. They are just fine. Mrs Ackart is somewhat bruised from the fall and will be sore from the operation for a few weeks. We will keep her in for a while until she has the staples out and then, if there are no complications, they can both go home."

"Oh that's wonderful news. Thank you, doctor." Rock said, shaking the doctor's hand enthusiastically.

Birch stared at Rock and the doctor unable to believe everything was alright, suddenly she was whisked up into Rock's arms and twirled around.

"Everything is alright, they are both alright." Rock said as he put Birch back down on the ground, an ecstatic smile spread across his face.

"Can we see them?" Rock asked.

"Mrs Ackart is still in recovery and is on heavy pain killers so it would be best to see her tomorrow, but you can certainly see your daughter now." The doctor said as he opened the door again. "I'll send in a nurse to show you the way to the nursery."

"Thank you, doctor...for everything." Rock said, relief washing over his face.

"You're very welcome." With one last smile the doctor left the room.

Birch and Rock happily hugged each other again.

Within a few minutes a nurse arrived to take Rock and Birch to the nursery. There were five babies in the nursery and the nurse went to one of the cots, picked up the tiny bundle wrapped in a blanket and handed it to Rock. He held the sleeping baby in his arms with a look of pure joy on his face. Sitting down in a nearby chair, he held her gently against him.

"Birch, come and meet your sister, Amber." Rock reached out one of his hands to Birch.

Birch slowly stepped forward and looked down at the little face in the blanket. She was so tiny and utterly beautiful.

"I have a sister?" She said.

Amber squirmed in her sleep as if in answer to her question and a little hand appeared as if from nowhere.

"Look how small her hands are...and her nails..." Birch said as her heart filled instantly with love. She knelt by the chair watching Amber's little face.

"Would you like to hold her?" Rock asked.

"Me? I don't know how." Birch said suddenly panicked, "What if I drop her?"

"You won't. Here..." Rock got up out of the chair, "Sit here and I will show you."

Birch sat down feeling more than a little nervous.

"You have to remember to support her head because she is not strong enough to do it herself yet. So one arm under her head." Rock placed Amber in Birch's arms, Amber's head resting on her elbow joint. "Now place that hand under her bottom and use your other arm to support underneath."

Birch did as instructed and was surprised at the weight of her, she was so small and yet seemed heavy. She could feel this warm, little wrapped up bundle next to her heart, she was so helpless and so beautiful that Birch was lost for words.

"Amazing, isn't she? To think your mum and I made her...made a human being."

"She is a miracle, isn't she?" Birch said.

"Yes, she is."

Eventually, Birch handed Amber back to Rock and he sat with her in his arms again not saying a word just staring down at her. When it was time to leave, they both went home in a contented and very relieved mood.

Early the next day, Elder Daisy popped in to check on Rock and Birch and to invite Birch over to Elder Violet's farm, which sat on the outskirts of the village. Lambing season had begun and she thought that Birch would be interested to see the new lambs.

During the fifteen-minute walk to the farm, Elder Daisy noticed how different Birch was from when she had seen her at the Imbolc rehearsal just a day before. She listened as Birch talked endlessly about her new sister with such pride in her voice that Elder Daisy didn't want to stop her.

Elders' Violet and Wolf's farm is a small farm with twenty or so sheep, a few goats and chickens and a large vegetable plot. Old farm buildings and muddy pathways surround the small stone cottage. Birch and Elder Daisy walked up one of the paths to the largest barn, their rubber boots squelching in the mud from the recent rain and their breath making clouds in the late January cold air.

The barn was only a little warmer than outside and it smelt of hay and animals. Half of the building was full of equipment and bags of feed, the other half was divided into several pens. Some had sheep in with their newly born lambs, others were empty, presumably waiting for their occupants.

Elder Violet was knelt on the straw in one of the pens with a very large sheep, which was laid quietly on its side. She was dressed in a deep blue overall with a purple jumper underneath that showed at the neck. She had rubber boots on as well and her long blonde hair was hidden in her blue and red stripped knitted hat. She looked up as Birch and Elder Daisy approached.

"Hello you two. You're just in time, this young lady is not far off lambing." She smiled showing her slightly crooked teeth, which didn't detract from her lovely face one bit.

Elder Daisy said 'Hello', she had picked up a spare bucket on the way through the barn and turned it upside down to sit on.

"Thank you for inviting me." Birch said politely as she rushed to the gate of the pen, "How many lambs have you got so far?" she said.

"We've got eight and that includes one set of twins. This one's got a lamb bleating for her in the pasture already. It was a late autumn lamb and she had recently weaned it off her milk, ready for this new one but the other lamb doesn't want to let go." Elder Violet stroked the rump of the sheep as it shuddered. "That's my girl, you're nearly there." She said to the sheep.

Birch seemed thoughtful while she watched the sheep's contractions get nearer together. "How will the other lamb manage without its mum?" She asked.

"Oh it'll be fine, it's already eating the feed we put out. I think it was a bit clingy because the mum was too busy trying to make herself strong for this little one and not taking much notice of it."

The prone sheep bleated again and tiny hoofs appeared at the sheep's rear end and, as the sheep pushed, more of the lamb could be seen until the last of the body and head rushed out with a sticky wet sound and plopped onto the straw. Elder Violet cleared its nose and mouth of the mucus just as the sheep reached round and began licking the lamb clean.

"Well done, girl." Elder Violet said to the sheep and backed away wiping her hands on a rag. She lent against the pen rails next to Elder Daisy and Birch.

"Aww...it's so cute." Birch said.

"You just watch, in a minute it will try to stand and feed." Elder Violet said.

As if the lamb had heard what she said, it began to try to stand on its wobbly, weak legs. It tried and tried for several minutes and eventually managed to get nearer to its mothers teats and hungrily began feeding with loud slurping noises.

Birch grinned with absolute pleasure. She was amazed at how quickly the lamb needed to feed and how hard it had tried to reach its mother's milk. She watched as the sheep continued to lick the lamb clean as it fed.

"We had best be getting back, Birch. I know Rock was anxious to get to the hospital to see how your mum and the baby are doing."

"Oh yes. I understand you have a lamb of your own now." Elder Violet said, "Congratulations on getting a sister."

Birch smiled proudly, "Thank you and thanks for letting me come over."

"You're very welcome, my dear. You can come over to visit the animals whenever you like. Tell your mum I'll pop over when she is back home and settled." With that Elder Violet waved them goodbye and turned back to her midwife duties.

Birch and Elder Daisy began the chilly walk back home. It seemed to Elder Daisy that Birch's thoughts were elsewhere on the return journey.

"You're quiet, Birch. Is everything alright?" Elder Daisy said.

"Oh yes, I'm fine. I was just thinking about the sheep's other lamb, the one out in the field."

"Oh? What about it?"

"It's kind of like me and mum, I think."

"How so, dear?" Elder Daisy watched Birch closely with a knowing look on her face.

"Well, I guess I've been a bit clingy just like it was...wanting mum's and Rock's attention when they were so busy getting ready for the baby. I don't think they were ignoring me after all, I think they were just trying to get everything right for when Amber arrived, just like the sheep was. Does that sound silly?"

"Oh no, not at all. I think you're very wise to see it that way and I know your mum would be very proud of you." Elder Daisy said as she put her arm around Birch and gave her a reassuring hug as they rounded the last corner.

"Look, there's Rock waiting for you by your front door, I think he's eager to get going. You run on ahead and tell your mum I will come and see her soon."

"Okay." Birch said as she began to run, she stopped and ran back to Elder Daisy and gave her a big hug.

"Oh, thank you. What did I do to deserve that?" She said jokingly.

"You helped me to put things straight in my head. Thank you." With one extra squeeze Birch turned and ran towards home.

Over the next few days Rock and Birch spent many happy hours at the hospital with her mum, who now had the baby beside her in a small portable cot in her room. Birch loved the idea of a sister more and more and by the time her mum and the baby were allowed home Birch was an utterly besotted with her new sister.

The evening of Imbolc had arrived and Birch was on the Goddess Mound preparing for the ritual with the rest of the village children. It's traditional in Brew, to celebrate Imbolc by having a ritual within the circle of thirteen stones on the Goddess Mound, a hillock that looks like a pregnant stomach. The stones had been upon the Goddess Mound for as long as anyone could remember and most of the 'turning of the wheel' seasonal celebrations were held there. Torches staked into the hard winter soil lit the entire mound in a soft glowing light.

The large crowd had begun to gather at the top of the Goddess Mound. Everyone knew his or her place. The Elders were stood within the ring of stones, one in front of each stone with the fire keeper tending the fire in the centre. The rest of the village stood outside the ring of stones forming a circle around them. The orange light from the torches shone on their expectant faces.

Birch and the rest of the children were standing on a small grassy flat area just off the main ritual space, they were blocked from view by the stones and the fact that the ground on which they stood was a little lower than the ritual space. Birch peaked over the edge and saw her mum sat in a wheel chair holding Amber and Rock stood behind her holding the handles of the chair. Her mum had not wanted to borrow a chair for the ritual but conceded when she realised that the steep climb of the Goddess Mound was a lot more painful than she had expected, having had her stomach muscles cut during the caesarean section, only one week before.

At last, a hush descended and everyone stilled waiting for the ritual to begin.

A slow rhythmic drumming began as the members of the local band Moon Scape began the opening ritual. As they drummed, from off to the right of the sacred space, the Elders stepped forward and their leader, Elder Bear, walked to the centre of the circle with Elder Daisy. Elder Bear is one of the nicest men that Birch knows, he is tall with a big beard and a lovely deep voice. He always seemed happy and usually had a smile on his face.

"Hail and welcome one and all to our celebration of Imbolc." He called out.

"Hail." The villagers replied.

Elder Daisy stepped forward, "At Imbolc we celebrate the stirring of new life all around us from the first signs of growth with the beautiful crocus on the village green to the new life of the lambs in our fields. It is a time of new beginnings, of new things started, of the formation of new ideas and of the returning light."

That was the queue for the children to come into the circle. Each one was dressed in white robes wearing a circlet of Ivy on their heads with a paper crocus flower as the centrepiece. Every child carried a lit white candle and formed an avenue from Elder Daisy and Elder Bear, who stood at the head of it, out towards the edge of the stone circle and the villagers.

"We have a very special Imbolc welcome this year. An Imbolc child. Could the child be brought forth, please?"

Birch moved from her spot in the line and walked down the avenue of children to the end, where her mum and Rock stood. Giving her candle to Rock, she took Amber in her arms. Birch lead her family back up the aisle walking slowly while Rock helped her mum to walk, she had refused to use the wheelchair for this part of the ritual and at last they approached the Elders.

"We have been blessed with yet another life in Brew and, as is our custom, at the nearest celebration to the birth of the new life, the child is presented to the village and claimed by one and all."

Birch handed the baby to Elder Daisy.

"This child is to be known as Amber daughter of Fleur and Rock and sister to Birch. She is now an honoured member of this village and as such she is a daughter to all here. May the Gods bring her peace and strength and may you all bless her long life with your wisdom and love. May she return the same to you all. Hail and welcome to the community of Brew, Amber."

"Hail Amber." The villagers replied and everyone cheered.

Elder Daisy returned Amber to the arms of her mum.

"Now, if everyone could come forward for their Imbolc blessing." Elder Bear said.

Elder Daisy gave the traditional blessing to Birch and her family and they slowly made their way round the circle back to their original places.

The rest of the villagers, each carrying an unlit candle, walked in family groups down the aisle of children towards the Elders. They split of into two lines, one walking past Elder Daisy and the other past Elder Bear. They were greeted and given the traditional Imbolc blessing by the Elder Leaders, 'May the returning light bring wisdom and peace to your home' and each of their candles were lit from the large white candle that sat on the stone alter.

Birch, having returned to her place in the line, watched as the rest of the villagers walked along the line and received their blessings. Her mind wandered to the sound of the drumming from the band and she seemed mesmerized by the candle flames all around her. She felt a warm feeling of happiness deep inside her that made her smile, despite the growing cold.

The rest of the ritual became a blur as Birch watched and half listened to the words and let them wash over her, she enjoyed the wonderful peace that had descended on her. Eventually, the ritual came to an end with a closing speech from Elder Daisy and Elder Bear. The children filed out of their lines to stand next to each of the thirteen elders as the closing cheer of 'Hail and Farewell' went up and everyone cheered and applauded.

The children dispersed into the crowd returning to their families just as Birch returned to her mother's side.

"That was wonderful, love. You looked lovely, too." Mum said.

"Thanks." Birch smiled down at her mum who was now sat back in the wheelchair for the tough trip down the steep hill.

Birch knew she hated it and as soon as they got to the bottom of the Goddess Mound her mum who get out of the chair and walk, albeit slowly.

"Yes, you did a great job, Birch." Rock said.

"Thanks." Birch smiled, relieved that everything went well and she didn't fall over with her candle and burn herself or anyone else.

"It's getting cold. I think it's time to go down and head for the feast at Elder Heather's house. Are you both ready?" Rock said as he took off the brakes on the chair and began to turn it around.

"Wait…" Birch said suddenly as she watched the rest of the villagers start the descent back down towards the village.

"What is it, love? Have you forgotten something?" Mum asked.

"No. I…I just wanted to say something…" Birch looked nervously down at her charm bracelet and began fiddling with the tiny silver horse her dad had given her years ago.

"It's okay, you can tell us anything, you know." Rock said with an encouraging smile.

"Of course you can, love. What is it?" Mum said.

"Well…I think I've been the second lamb for a while…" Birch said.

"Second lamb? What do you mean?" Mum said as she reached out to hold Birch's hand with a confused look on her face.

"When I went to Elders Violet's farm to see the lambs being born, she told me about a lamb who still bugged it's mum even though she was trying to get ready for the new lamb that was about to be born. It pestered her and became selfish for her attention and…I think I've been like that. I'm sorry, I didn't mean to be selfish." Birch said as tears found their way down her cold pink cheeks.

"Aww sweetheart, don't cry. Come here...." Mum said as she held out the one arm that wasn't holding Amber reaching for a hug. "I know I've not been well enough during my pregnancy to help you with everything like I usually do and I'm sorry if you felt left out. You will always be my little miracle, no matter how big you get. I love you very much, you know."

"I love you too, mum." Birch hugged her mum hard, taking care not to crush Amber.

Birch felt Rock's arm around her too as he said, "I promised you that everything would be alright, didn't I?"

"Yes, you did." Birch said as she hugged him too. "One last thing..."

"Yes?" Both Rock and Fleur said at the same time.

"Amber will be calling you dad, won't she? Can I call you dad too?" She said as she smiled shyly at him.

"Of course you can!" He grinned broadly and gave her a huge hug, "I would be honoured for you to call me dad." His eyes looked extra sparkly and wet in the light of the torches.

"I'm so proud of you, love." Mum said as she kissed Birch nosily on the cheek.

Birch returned the kiss and said cheerily, "Is it time for hot chocolate and some of Hazel's mum's chocolate muffins yet?"

"Absolutely!" Rock said as he began to push the wheelchair across the grass. They headed down the steep winding path of the Goddess Mound back towards the village.

Birch walked beside them and helped negotiate the chair over the various lumps and bumps of the pathway. She watched her mum and dad as they made their way down. They looked so happy as they smiled at each other and smiled at Birch, chatting away excitedly about the coming feast. Birch's heart swelled with happiness because at last she felt like she had found her family once again.

Ash the Solitary Witch

An Introduction to Ash

Each of the children of Brew, have been named after items in Nature and Ash is no exception. Named after the Ash tree, which is also referred to as Yggdrasil in the Norse Tradition of Northern Europe and is the world tree. The Ash was also very sacred to the druids. Its main symbolism being that of stability as it links the inner and other worlds, it is also known as the wood of strength with penetrating and firm roots and connects the mundane with the spiritual.

Ash is a solitary girl, afraid of being disliked by others and always stayed away from anyone whom she thought wouldn't like her. This, of course, led to her having almost no friends, other than her dog Rufus. Although, she does have a very strong bond with her parents.

Ash is eleven years old, with very long blond hair and pale blue eyes. She has a small brown birthmark on her upper left cheek that is shaped like a tiny cloud, which she loves. Ash is of average height for her age and has a medium build.

Our tale begins a few days before the Spring Equinox, otherwise known as Ostara. This is a time when the growing season begins anew in full force and the Earth is in balance with the Sun making the days and nights the same length.

Ash the Solitary Witch

The bright spring sunshine glinted off the windows of the car. The dark green Volvo was parked in the drive and every last bit of space was packed with the family's belongings. Ash squinted at the reflection of the sun and climbed on the back seat. There was only just enough room for her as she squeezed in next to the boxes of books, the dog basket sat on the seat next to her and the half used bottles of pottery slip and tools in the space at her feet.

Dad opened the front passenger door and carefully climbed into the passenger seat, gingerly trying not to hit his leg, not an easy thing to do when your leg is in plaster.

"You can move the seat back, if you need more room, Dad." Ash said and smiled bravely, knowing full well that there wasn't much room for her legs already.

"I am okay. Thanks, Ash." Dad said through gritted teeth, "I will get comfy in a moment. I guess Rufus is holding your Mum up." He finally got into a comfy position and reached over to close the door.

"Yeah, I think Rufus is as nervous as me." She looked out of the window to see if she could see her Mum or Rufus.

"I know you're nervous about starting at your new school but at least you like the new house and the village. You will soon make some friends and enjoy school." Dad said, trying to sound positive.

"I know...but it just creeps up on me sometimes, without warning. Kind of like that mean old cat of Mrs Burbridges. Every time I walked past her house, on the way home from school, it leaps out and tries to bite me...horrid thing." Said Ash.

"Well, you're obviously such a tasty morsel that Berty just had to have a nibble!" Dad chuckled.

With a rush of cool morning air, Ash's door opened and in jumped a flash of warm gingery brown. Rufus, the mad Terrier, had decided he would spend the journey on Ash's lap, which was a good job really, as there was nowhere else for him to squeeze in.

"Sit down, you silly dog!" Ash squealed with joy as Rufus buried his nose in her long blonde hair and snuffled her ear. Rufus was her best friend and had been since she was two years old.

Mum climbed into the driver's seat and fastened her seat belt. "Hold on to him Ash, make sure he's safe." She turned to her husband, "He should really be in the back of the car, in a cage or something but there just isn't any room." She started the car with one turn of the key and it roared into life. "Well everyone, say your goodbyes to the house and the city and a big hello to our new life in the countryside!" With a huge smile she moved the car slowly down the short driveway and onto the main road.

Ash lovingly stroked Rufus on his favourite spot, behind the ears, and looked back over her shoulder at their old house. She felt like she was looking for a sign that she'd lived there, as she looked at each of the two story windows.

The house was in the middle of a row of identical houses. Still, it was her home and where she had found the best day-dreams, played with Rufus for hours and felt happier there than anywhere else in the city. Ash couldn't help feeling sad as the house got smaller and smaller until they turned the corner and it was suddenly gone.

Like it never existed.

Ash tried to remember what the new house looked like, it had been two months since they visited it. Two months, since her parents had decided to make the 'big change' and move permanently to the country. Ash's parents had been talking about doing this for many years and, when her Dad broke his leg at work, the compensation he got was the push they needed to get on with it. To Ash's parents this wasn't a project, it was a life long dream of living off the land as the Ancestors had done.

Once the plaster was off, Dad's leg would never be totally whole again. Due to the multiple breaks, the metal plates, pins and rods, he would always have a slight limp and probably have to use a cane. Dad had often said it was one of the best things that had happened to him. Now he could begin his dream of living off the land and concentrate more on his writing. His latest trilogy had been accepted by a publisher just the month before and he had been given a large cheque, although Ash did not know how large, he was very excited by it.

Ash's mum was looking forward to expanding her pottery business and running it from the outbuilding at the new house. She was also looking forward to having a real garden, not some small 'stamp sized' plot as she called their old garden, which was only big enough for a few tubs. She wanted a garden that she could really get her hands dirty working in and grow all the vegetables and herbs that the family would need to live on and perhaps even a few chickens.

Mum glanced in her rear view mirror, "You okay, Ash?"

Ash looked up at her Mum. It always felt like she was looking in a mirror, her Mum's eyes were exactly the same shade of blue as Ash's.

"Yeah, just a bit sad leaving our old home behind and...a bit...nervous about starting in a new school." Ash said while rubbing Rufus's tummy.

"That's natural, sweetie. I'm sure, once we've been there a few days, you will have found some new friends even before school starts again, after the Ostara break." Mum flashed a grin in the mirror as she turned off the main road and onto a narrow country lane. "You will probably find people of your own age at the Ostara Celebration the village is holding on Saturday too, I bet the whole village will be there. I am really looking forward to it."

"I'm looking forward to it, too." Said Dad, "It will be nice to have a chance to get to know our new neighbours."

"It gives us three days in the new house to get a bit sorted, then we can go out and celebrate." Mum said as she smiled happily at Dad.

Ash looked at her parents moodily, well at least they were happy about the move. "How long before we get there?" She asked, not feeling the excitement they were.

"It will take about an hour, unless your Dad gets too uncomfortable and we need to stop." Mum pulled over to the side of the narrow road to let a truck pass and then pulled back onto the road and continued on, "The movers should be there soon. They'll have moved the furniture in and hopefully put my kiln and wheel in the out building by the time we get there."

"I'm glad we hired some movers this time, especially with me out of commission. Some of the furniture is very heavy." Dad said, obviously happy he didn't have to struggle with it.

"We'll have the picnic lunch as soon as we arrive, then unpack the car and the trailer. That's if these bumpy roads don't disconnect it from us first." Laughed Mum.

Ash spun her head round trying to see the trailer but she couldn't see past all the boxes and bags in the back. "Are we losing it?" she asked worriedly.

"No, sweetie, I was just being silly. It's securely fastened, don't worry. You have to stop being so serious, you will love our new life in Brew. I know you will."

Ash looked down while she stroked Rufus, "Is it true?" Ash asked quietly.

"Is what true, Ash?" Dad said.

"I was wondering, is it true that everyone who lives there are like us, followers of The Old Ways? Are they all Witches?"

"Ah...yes, it's true. It's not like in the city where many folks have forgotten or lost interest in The Old Ways. In Brew, everyone is a witch and we will have a lot in common with the villagers straight away. Won't that make a nice change?" He said.

"Yes, I guess...it'll be nice to have someone my age, who knows what I am talking about." Ash said. That's if they will like a city girl, she thought to herself, knowing she was going to feel out of place and already dreading it.

In town, there had been only two other families, who lived near them, that were of The Old Ways. Neither had any children the same age as her, they were either much older or very young. Ash had never really had friends to share the celebrations with and was nervous about her possible new ones. Still, she really wished they weren't moving. She had liked things just as they were, even if she had no one her age to enjoy the Festival Days with, apart from Rufus that is and, seeing as he was her best friend, what more could she need?

Yes, she decided...she did just fine on her own, just her and Rufus. Just fine. Nothing needed to change, she didn't need friends. She would be happy in the new house, just her and Rufus...as it always had been. Rufus, and her dreams of living alone and playing in the woods. Images of her running with Rufus in the bright sunshine in some quiet woods, tumbled through her mind as she closed her eyes against the bright sunshine and daydreamed.

"Ash...wake up. Ash?" Mum's voice softly called, her hand gently shaking Ash's shoulder. "We have arrived. You feel asleep, sweetie."

Ash opened her eyes and slowly the blurry image changed into her Mums lovely freckled face with Ash's eyes. "Are we here already? I think I slept the whole way." Rufus realising she was waking up, jumped down and out of the car. He started to sniff around, soon he vanished behind a bush in the front garden.

Mum stood up, "Yup, we're here at last!" Smiling, Mum helped Dad out of the car and then headed off to talk to the movers and check the right pieces were in the right rooms before paying them.

Ash rubbed her eyes and climbed out of the car, she stood in the light breeze, looking at her new home. Quickly scooping back behind an ear the hair that was blown in her face, Ash looked around. The cottage itself was a lovely, built from stone with a thatched roof and the upstairs windows poked through the thatch. The entire front of the cottage was covered in a climbing rose that was just beginning to bud.

The front garden was half a flower garden with a big apple tree and half gravel drive. The drive led down the side of 'Rose Cottage' to the back garden with a small green house, a garage and the old outhouse. The outhouse would be mum's new pottery studio and where the mover's van was now parked.

Ash had to admit it was a beautiful cottage and she looked forward to smelling the lovely honeysuckle and jasmine that grew around the wooden front door, which was, at present, propped open with a fire extinguisher while the movers moved in and out.

Rufus ambled over and stood by Ash's leg, she picked him up and hugged him, "Well, Rufus? It's very pretty, isn't it?" Ash rubbed his ear, "Perhaps we can get used to it, what do you say?" Ash looked in his eyes and jumped as he suddenly barked.

"Hello?"

An unknown voice called from behind Ash and made Rufus bark again. Ash spun round to see a girl about her age, standing near the front fence.

"Hello." Ash answered shyly as she held on tightly to Rufus and tried to hush him.

"Are you moving in?" The girl asked.

"Yes, we've just arrived." Ash walked down the short drive and stood near the gate, feeling a little awkward and self-conscious. Just a couple of feet away from the pretty girl with long brown hair, bright blue eyes and a slightly bent nose. She was dressed in jeans and a multi-coloured sweater.

"My name's Holly. I live round the corner near the pub and the bakers." Holly said with a friendly smile.

"I'm Ash and this rascal is Rufus, the Mad Terrier." Ash laughed as Rufus sniffed Holly and let her stroke him.

"He is lovely. It's nice to meet you both. We don't get new people around here very often, I'm glad that someone is moving into Elder Rose's cottage, it's been empty for a while." Holly smiled, "I was just on my way to my friend Yew's house, which is four houses that way." Holly pointed down the lane that ran past the front of Ash's new home. "Would you like to come and meet her?" Holly asked hopefully.

"Erm...No, I can't." Ash blushed and looked down at Rufus "I have to help my mum."

"Oh, okay. Well you'll meet her and everyone else on Saturday at the Ostara Celebration. You are coming, aren't you?" Holly asked while she was already walking away.

"Yep, we are planning to." Ash replied.

"Great. See you then, Bye." Holly waved and disappeared behind the row of trees down the lane.

"Well, she was in a hurry." Mumbled Ash to Rufus. "Couldn't get away from me fast enough. Do I have a big sign on my head that says 'stupid city girl'?" Ash grumpily headed towards the house just as her mum was coming out, saying goodbye to the movers.

"Thank you." Mum called out to the moving men as they backed out of the drive and pulled away. She turned to Ash, "Time for some lunch. Will you help me unpack the cool boxes from the car?"

"Sure." Putting Rufus down on the gravel, Ash headed with her mum to the back of the car.

"Did I hear you talking to someone, sweetie?" Mum asked.

"Oh yeah, a girl called Holly came and said hello, she rushed off real fast though. Probably hates city folk." Ash grabbed one of the two cool boxes and the flask.

"I'm sure that's not the case, she was probably just busy or even late for something. You must try not to jump to conclusions about people and things you do not know." Mum replied with a smile, picked up the other cool box.

"I don't want friends who think I am a stupid city girl. I'm happy with just me and Rufus." Ash started walking towards the cottage.

"Ash, listen to me..." Said mum as she caught up with her. "We all need friends...others to talk to about...anything with. It kind of makes things easier to understand and deal with, if we talk to people who know us and love us." Mum placed her hand on Ash's arm making them both stop walking.

"I do have people I can talk to and who love me, I have you and Dad and Rufus." Ash looked at her Mum.

"Of course you have us sweetie but one day you will want others of your own age and you'll enjoy their company, even more than Rufus's." Mum laughed.

"Not likely." Ash chuckled, "You three are the best."

"Of course we are." Laughed mum, "I'm starving, let's go create a masterpiece of food." Mum headed through the front door and Ash followed closing the front door behind her wondering if her mum was right. Would she need friends here? Or even want them?

She followed her mum as she walked down the wood panel hallway, past the doorway to the living room on the left and the stairs on the right, into the Kitchen with the old fashioned range. Dad was sat at the big oak table they had brought from the old house, he had his bad leg propped up on a cushion on one of the dining chairs.

It was warm in the kitchen, dad had lit the range and thrown logs in already. Ash and her mum emptied out the cool boxes and sat down to sandwiches, cold sausages, cheese, small tomatoes and fruit.

"Can you unpack the books and put them on the library shelves in the living room, love, if I group all the boxes around you? You won't have to move around much and it will give us some space to relax in later?" Mum asked Dad.

"Sure can. I also want to make room around my desk by the front window so I can sit and work there until this darned plaster comes off. I have a feeling there is another book coming." Dad laughed and mum reached over to kiss him.

"That's great. I'll sort our bedroom and then the kitchen after lunch." Mum turned to Ash. "Will you help me unpack the kitchen after you have sorted your bedroom?" She asked.

"Yup, Rufus and I will help." Ash smiled and picked up another cold sausage. She broke the end off and secretly gave it to Rufus under the table. Her Mum didn't like him being fed from the table, especially when they were eating.

"Thanks, sweetie." Mum sat back in her chair, stretched and smiled. "I can't believe we are finally here, I can't wait to start working again and get to know the village and the people. We're here just at the right time of year too, we can plant out some of the seedlings we brought with us. That reminds me, as soon as I've finished eating, I'll transfer the seedlings to the little greenhouse to keep them warm."

Once everyone had finished lunch, Mum helped dad to start emptying the boxes of books onto the wooden shelves in the living room and Ash quickly tidied the leftovers back into the coolers and headed up the stairs to her new room. She had seen it once before but it had been full of the previous owners junk boxes and old furniture.

The door of her room was open wide and the sun streamed in through the window, directly opposite the door. As Ash's eyes adjusted to the brightness, she saw all her boxes on the floor and her bed against the wall on her right with her shelves standing behind the door, on the left wall was her wardrobe, her desk and a built in cupboard. The ceiling was slanted on the right hand side due to the slope of the thatched roof.

Ash moved across the room, around the boxes to her window and opened it wide, letting in the gentle warmth of the early spring day and fresh air. The air here was lovely and clean, it didn't smell of exhaust like at the old house. Here, it was fresh and smelt nice. Ash took a few deep breaths and sighed happily. Yes, she thought, Rufus and I will be happy here after all.

"Well, at least my room is nice even if it does need painting." She said out loud to Rufus just as he jumped on her bed.

"Silly, it has no covers on yet, you can't snuggle up and go to sleep." Rufus ignored her and turned around several times before finding a good spot on the mattress and lay down. He stayed there watching Ash move about the room taking books, candles, jewellery and clothes out of the boxes and start arranging them on shelves, in drawers and on hangers.

That night, Ash lay in bed listening to an owl hooting in a near by tree, it was amazingly quiet at night here. There was no shouting in the street nor any cars whizzing by or trucks thundering past. There was none of those city noises, just the sound of the owl and an occasional bark from a fox.

Ash drifted off into a relaxed sleep and before long dreams took over and led her away into another world.

She awoke suddenly in the middle of the night drenched with sweat from a frightening dream. Ash didn't have to try to remember the dream, it was the same one she'd had for many years. She had dreamt of her 'dream family', as she liked to call them. In this dream, her 'dream family' were celebrating a birthday when a big storm had blown up and swept everyone but her away, leaving her alone in the dark.

There was no point telling her parents she'd had the dream again. She had dreamt it so often before, that they had taken her to a special doctor who had decided it was a result of Ash's sister dying, just after she had been born, on the very day that Ash had held her for the first time. It wasn't Ash's fault of course, the baby had died from a 'heart problem', but still, Ash felt like her family wasn't complete and she longed for a large family with lots of brothers and sisters.

Over time, it seemed that there would only ever be Ash and Rufus and she had gotten used to the idea, but every now and then, the dream would come back and make Ash sad and lonely.

By the time Saturday came, every room in the house had been sorted out and cleaned, even though it needed some painting and new carpets, the cottage now felt like home to Ash and her family.

"Do I have to go?" Asked Ash, for the second time that day.

"Yes, you do. We have all been so busy with the house for the last few days that today is a day off. We are going to celebrate Ostara with the rest of the village and have some fun." Mum said and smiled determinedly, while handing Ash her fleece.

"Okay, okay. If I have too..." She pulled on her fleece and zipped it up, "...but don't expect me to talk to anyone I don't know and that's everyone." Ash said, looking defeated.

"Ash, you will do fine. Maybe that girl you met, Holly was it? Maybe she'll be there." Said dad as he zipped up his jacket and lent on his crutches, watching Mum pick up the picnic basket and blanket.

"Yes, her name was Holly, but I don't know if she'll want a weirdo from the city hanging about." Ash replied and picked up the bag containing the two flasks full of hot chocolate. She grabbed Rufus's lead off the hook by the door and fastening it to his collar.

"I'm sure she'll be glad you see you, sweetie and you're not a weirdo." Said mum sternly as she opened the front door and let everyone out.

They walked down the lane towards the centre of the village. There were bright yellow flags strung across from one telephone pole to the next, encircling the village green and the shops. The shops had big signs saying 'Happy Ostara' and 'Ostara Blessings' in every window. As the family walked past the bakers, they saw bread loaves in the window baked in the shapes of the Sun, Hares and Eggs.

Ash's family followed the other people down the short lane toward a place that was signed posted as the 'Goddess Mound', more and more people joined the walk, all of them stopping to say hello and introduce themselves. By the time they reached the base of the mound Ash's mind was whirling with the new names and faces she had met along the way, but all of this vanished when she saw the Mound and gasped.

The Goddess Mound had steep sides with winding path to the top and on top stood thirteen majestic stones in a circle. Ash stood and gapped, she had never seen anything so powerful and beautiful in her entire life.

"Lovely, isn't it?" Mum whispered in Ash's ear.

"Wow, I didn't know this was here." She said.

"This is where the villagers of Brew have every Festival Day Celebration and every special event. I thought you would like it." Mum smiled, kissed Ash's cheek and headed towards the start of the spiral path with dad hobbling along beside her.

Ash followed her parents and the crowd as they all moved up the winding path to the top. She looked around and was surprised and enchanted yet again. At the top everyone was stood around the stones but on the outside of the circle, waiting.

In the middle was a large man with a long beard tending to the fire, around him were thirteen men and woman all robed in long bright yellow robes, each one stood in front of one of the standing stones forming the circle. Off to the right was what looked like a band, men and women with guitars and drums, who sat quietly on folding chairs, also waiting. Ash looked around the circle at the people, there must have been a couple of hundred people stood outside the stones. All of them were hushed looking toward the people inside.

Ash continued to look around the circle, she spotted Holly just as Holly looked at her and before Ash could look away shyly, Holly waved and smiled. Ash returned the wave with a shy smile and noticed that Holly was stood with a group of other girls about the same age who all looked over at Ash and also waved and smiled. Ash blushed bright red as she waved back but was unable to smile as she was instantly furious with herself for blushing so much. Before Ash could try to hide her embarrassment by looking away, one of the people inside the circle stepped inward, towards the fire and everyone turned their eyes to him.

"Welcome everyone to our Blessed Celebration of Ostara." The man called out in a deep, thick voice that rumbled out of him, through his big bushy brown beard and into the air. "Every year, at the Spring Equinox, we gather at this sacred place to honour the balance between day and night and the continuance of spring and re-growth that started at Imbolc in February."

Ash relaxed knowing she was not the centre of the girls' attention anymore and looked down at Rufus, who loved being with lots of people. He sat happily at Ash's feet, looking around him and sniffing the air.

"In the spirit of balance and re-growth, I would like to welcome the newcomers to our village; Lilly, Thorn and their daughter Ash with her dog Rufus." The man called out and moved across the circle.

Ash's attention snapped back into place as she realised he was talking about her family and was walking over to them. She was horrified and blushed even more.

"Welcome to Brew." He said as he offered his hand to mum and dad. "I'm Elder Bear, co-leader of the Elders of Brew." He said and put his hand out to Ash.

Timidly, Ash looked up into the big mans eyes and saw such happiness and kindness there that she shook his hand without thinking about it. His grip was as warm and gentle as his smile.

"Welcome Ash, welcome to you all." His voice boomed and a big cheer went up from the crowd.

Ash was so stunned by this introduction she barely noticed the crowd cheering and looking her and her family. What a nice man, was all she could think.

Elder Bear walked back toward the other Elders and stood next to a tall thin lady. She began to talk about the meaning of the Spring Equinox and how the balance of the Equinox should be reflected in your own lives, by finding balance in all that you do. Elder Bear and the tall lady, together with the other Elders then began to make offerings to the Goddess by sprinkling grains on the ground around the inner circle and at the base of each stone, they then pouring an offering of Mead into the flames of the fire.

Ash watched the ritual with enthusiasm as she had never attended such a large celebration. The small ones she used to go to, with her parents in the city, were usually held in some-one's living room and even though there were only two other families, the room had always been full and uncomfortably hot with no room to move about.

Within moments the Elders burst into song and after the first verse the band joined in, as did the people outside the cir-cle.

Ash was amazed as joy filled her heart at the beauty of the song and how everyone happily joined in. She'd never been to a ritual like this. Ash glanced at her parents who were holding hands and smiling, obviously enjoying this new way to cele-brate. Ash looked round at the crowd to see if Holly and the group of girls were all singing too but they were not there. Not one of them. In fact, all the children who had been stood around the stones, had gone. Ash looked around quickly to try and spotted them, but there was no sign of them. Perhaps they all got bored and just left, she thought. But how could they get bored of this? She wondered.

Ash could hear another rhythm building in the music, another drum beat that didn't fit with the rest but intertwined inside the music, she look over at the band and two of the drummers were building a different beat. The song came to an end but the extra rhythm of the drums continued and then a burst of singing rang out between the stones. Ash looked round to see who was singing but no one was.

As she watched the crowd parted slightly as a string of children, all holding hands, each dressed in robes of pale yellow, blue, pink and green began dancing in a line weaving in and out of the Elders, the stones and around the fire pit singing loudly as they went.

"Blessings of the Balance, Blessings of the Green. We give our thanks, for everything that's been."

They sang as they weaved around.

"Blessings of the Flowers, Blessings of the Sun. We have hope, for everything to come."

Their voices rang out, as they got closer to Ash and her family.

"Blessings of the Old."

The string of children was now in front of Ash.

Holly held out her hand for Ash to join them and smiled as everyone sang, "Blessings of the New. We give our Blessings, to everyone of you."

Ash took a deep breath, quickly looked at her parents who nodded and smiled, and before she knew what she was doing she had passed mum Rufus' lead, taken Holly's hand and joined the string of children as they went on their way around the circle.

Again everyone cheered and sang with the children as they accepted their new friend.

Ash held Holly's hand tightly and the unknown boy's hand, who was directly behind her, without even looking at him. She followed Holly with her heart beating wildly as they repeated the song.

"Blessings of the Balance, Blessings of the Green."

"We give our thanks, for everything that's been."

"Blessings of the Flowers, Blessings of the Sun."

"We have hope, for everything to come."

"Blessings of the Old, Blessings of the New."

"We give our Blessings, to everyone of you."

The string found its way into the middle of the circle of Elders and went around the fire one last time and then stopped. The children all stood with their hands in the air and shouted, "Blessing of Ostara to you all!"

Everyone clapped and cheered and moved into the stone circle hugging each other. Holly hugged Ash, "Welcome to Brew, Ash." She said with a huge smile, "I hope you didn't mind joining in, the song and dance is a tradition here to welcome new children to the dance. I'm sorry I didn't get chance to warn you the other day, I was late dropping off medicine to Yew's Grandma." She smiled.

Ash was suddenly relieved to hear the reason why Holly had rushed off and that it wasn't because of her. Ash's Mum had been right after all. Although she was still breathless from the excitement, she managed to say, "It was fun. If I'd known before...I'd probably have worried about it anyway." She smiled shyly.

"No need to worry, we're all friendly here." Holly grinned, "It's like one big happy family, you'll love it."

Ash's heart leapt as a warm feeling of coming home spread through her. Her longing to be part of big family had finally come true. She smiled at Holly, "You know, I think I will love it here."

"Feel like meeting some new friends?" Holly asked offering her hand again.

Ash looked at it and at Holly's smiling face. She bravely placed her hand in Holly's, "Okay but can we get Rufus first? I kind of threw his lead at mum when I went to dance with you."

"Sure, it would be nice to see him again." Holly said.

They made their way through the celebrating crowd, who were either stood about in groups chatting or sat sharing picnics.

As Ash lead the way back to her parents, who were stood by one of the stones, her Dad was leaning on it for support, she could tell she felt different inside. She looked around at the crowd and realised that everyone here was acting as one big 'family'. She realised that you don't need to be of the same blood to be part of a family, you just need to feel loved and safe, and she did. Ash got a sudden flash of her 'dream family' all smiling at her and now there were others stood around her, including Holly and Elder Bear and many other villagers she had meet that morning. The flash ended and she could feel the dream and the loneliness, she had always felt inside, melt away.

It was amazing, she felt like she had known Holly forever, almost like a sister.

Her parents were talking to Elder Bear and several others when Holly and Ash arrived. They looked so happy, laughing with their new friends. Rufus jumped up at Ash as she got close and everyone laughed at him.

Ash glanced at all their new friends and how happy everyone looked to have them in the village. "This is Holly, Mum."

"Hello." Holly said with a big smile on her face.

"Hello Holly, it is very nice to meet you." Mum said and began asking Holly about the dancing.

Ash smiled to herself as she bent down and whispered to Rufus, "Maybe we came here at the right time after all. Maybe the balance of the Spring Equinox has helped to balance everything inside me. It looks like the move and the balance of friends and family is a thing good after all, Rufus. I think we'll be much happier here than we first thought." Ash took a deep breath full of courage and pure happiness and looked up at her Mum. "I'm off to make some new friends, Mum." Ash said as she picked up Rufus and stood up, "See you later."

Mum smiled and winked at Ash.

Ash grinned back and, with a feeling of completeness, she walked off into the crowd with Holly at her side and Rufus in her arms.

Willow the Lonely Witch

An Introduction to Willow

All the children of Brew have been named after things in Nature and Willow is no exception.

She is named after the Willow tree, which is regarded as feminine and is closely associated with the moon and water. It's seen as a melancholic tree representing sadness, it is believed sitting underneath it will soothe the emotions and banish depression and sadness. In addition, it is associated to love, healing, rhythms, and the gaining of eloquence, inspiration, growth and skills.

Willow is an ordinary girl, who loves to swim and dreams of being on the school swim team like her best friend Rowan. They are equally talented but when it came to Willow's chance she was so distracted by the events earlier in her day that she didn't do her best time and missed out on being on the team.

Willow is the younger of two children and is eleven years old, with shoulder length fair hair and pale green eyes. She has a slim build, average height and is excellent at maths. She misses her brother, Marsh who is away at college, very much. She feels very alone when she hears some life changing news. Can she struggle through alone? Does she have to? Are her fears valid and real, or imaginings of a lonely girl?

Our tale begins two weeks before the Beltane, which is a time to celebrate fertility and it's during this festival that Handfastings, a Pagan version of marriage, are sometimes held.

Willow the Lonely Witch

Willow sat on a bench at the edge of the school pool, wrapped in a towel. She was watching the swim team do their lengths with a sadness in her heart, she had just 'tried out' for the team, but knew she hadn't done as well as she'd liked. Her time was too far behind the others and she hadn't made the team. It wasn't that she wasn't good enough, normally she was able to get very good times, hence why she'd been given a chance to try for the team. In fact, she had once beaten the time of their lead swimmer and Willow's best friend, Rowan, but not today.

Today was already a bad day, now it was worse.

She wondered, as she sat miserably wrapped in her towel, if she could ask the swim coach for another try. Willow knew she was distracted by the news that her mum had given her this morning.

Willow had been sat at the breakfast table eating her cereal when her mum, April, had announced that her girlfriend, Hana, would be moving in with them and they were going to get Handfasted at Beltane. Willow had met Hana several times and liked her, but she knew that she would be the only student at school with two mums and this thought terrified her.

Willow forced her thoughts back to the swimming pool and her 'try out' failure just a few moments before. She sat angrily rubbing dry her wet hair, unable to focus on the swim team's practise. How was she going to tell her friends about her two mums? Everyone would laugh at her and call her names. Why couldn't her mum be like everyone else's? It just wasn't fair.

"You okay?"

Willow looked up, from staring at the tiled ground around the pool, to see her best friend Rowan. Rowan pulled off her swimming cap and ruffled her hand through her short curly brown hair. Her big brown eyes looked down at Willow concerned.

"Yeah." Willow said.

"What's the matter? You seem distracted, is it because your time was a bit slow? I'm sure the coach will give you another chance, if you ask." Rowan said helpfully as she sat down next to Willow on the wooden bench.

Willow looked up at the glass ceiling of the pool enclosure wondering what to say. She couldn't tell people about her mum Handfasting Hana, what would they think? No, this was something she had to keep to herself.

"Yeah, it was a rubbish time. I guess my mind is elsewhere." Willow stood up holding her towel in her hands.

"Are you going to talk to Coach Ruby?" Rowan said.

"Not now...I...I'll see you later." Willow quickly turned and walked away. She headed for the changing rooms leaving Rowan looking worriedly after her.

The team tryouts were after the last lesson of the day and the school was quiet and empty when Willow had finished getting changed and began the walk home. The walk wasn't a long one, but she walked it slowly not wanting to get home. She decided to delay her journey by walking the alternative route, which took much longer. The pathway led her by the river and the woods before twisting back into the village.

As Willow walked along, she listened to the birds singing in the late afternoon sunshine and the sound of the water. She loved the river and listened as the water tumbled over the stones and rocks on its way past her. These sights and sounds had always managed to sooth her whenever she had felt the need to be on her own.

At last she saw it, the one thing she had loved as long as she could remember.

Grandmother Willow, the largest weeping willow she had ever seen. Her gentle waving arms were reaching out and stroking the water. Willow had named the tree Grandmother Willow when she had been very small. It always felt like visiting a wonderful and very old grandmother, when she came here. The secret place within the tree was still hidden even as the warm spring breeze moved the leaves and branches.

Willows steps quickened as she drew near, she gently moved aside the long leafy branches to reveal the heart of the tree. The huge trunk towered above her and the space within the branches was approximately eight feet in circumference around the trunk. This special place was completely enclosed by the tree's hanging branches. Inside, there was a large rock, which the tree had grown around. It made for an excellent seat and it was Willow's favourite spot.

Being enclosed in this special and private place usually made Willow feel safe and almost held by the tree, as if it reached out with its long thin arms and hugged her.

Today was different.

Although, Willow still felt safe and loved, she also felt a terrible sense of loneliness. She knew that she couldn't talk to her mum about her worries as it would upset her and she knew that her friends would all look at her as if she had a strange disease or two heads if she told them she was going to have two mums soon.

Willow sighed deeply.

Never, in her entire life, had she ever felt this alone. She had wondered about ringing her brother, but she knew that he was very busy at college and would have not time for her 'silliness'. The age gap of six years meant they usually had nothing in common with each other, but she still missed him greatly.

Willow sat and watched the branches sway in the breeze, brushing the surface of the water. She seemed to stare at the movement for hours, hoping that she could just stay here, where no one would laugh at her or avoid her for being different. Why couldn't her mum realise how hard this was going to make things for Willow and just not get Handfasted? Willow knew she was being selfish, but couldn't stop her mind thinking it. She just couldn't see any other way out.

"What am I going to do, Grandmother Willow?" She asked the rustling leaves.

Grandmother Willow's reply was a continued silence punctuated with the gentle swishing noises of the branches.

Willow sat in silence for a long time letting the sound of the willow leaves, river and the birds wash over her, forcing her brain not to think.

Willow's stomach rumbled loudly and she sighed again.

It was time to go home, her mum would wonder where she was if she didn't get home soon and swimming always made her hungry. With a bone deep reluctance, Willow swept back the concealing curtain of weeping branches and, with a quick glance back she mentally said 'goodbye' to Grandmother Willow and she once again joined the path that would lead her home.

Willow's home was a small semi-detached stone cottage on the outskirts of the village. It had three rooms downstairs; the lounge, bathroom and kitchen, whilst upstairs there were three small bedrooms.

Willow walked up the gravel path and stood for a moment looking at her front door. She wasn't seeing the peeling blue paint or the old splits in the wood. No, she was trying to summon up the courage to open it.

She could smell dinner and hear laughter from within, but she felt as shut out and left in the cold as if the door had actually been closed in her face.

Taking a deep breath, she grabbed the door handle and forced herself to go in.

The smell of dinner was wonderful and made her stomach growl instantly.

"Willow? Is that you, love?" Her mum called.

"Yes, mum." She replied as she hung up her coat and school bag.

"Dinner's ready." Mum said as Willow walked into the kitchen.

The kitchen held a small table where the family ate all their meals. Willow sat at her place at the table after saying hello to Hana. Hana smiled, said and signed 'hello' back. Hana was small and redheaded, with small almost pixie like features. She had been born partially deaf and could lip-read extremely well, she had been teaching Willow how to sign for the last couple of months.

Willow signed 'Hello' back and took a sip of water from the glass set before her.

"How was your day?" Mum asked.

"Long." Willow said without looking up from her glass. She could almost feel her Mum and Hana exchange looks of surprise.

"Everything okay, love?" Mum said as she laid a hand on Willow's shoulder.

"I didn't make the swim team."

"Oh Willow, I am sorry." Mum said as she reached down and hugged Willow, "I didn't realise you were trying for it today, why didn't you say so?"

Willow shrugged feeling embarrassed.

'What happened?" Hana asked.

"My time was too slow, just having a bad day I guess." Willow said.

"Can you ask for a retest?" Mum asked.

"Rowan thinks I can. I might ask Coach Ruby tomorrow, see if she'll let me."

"I'm sure she will, she knows how hard you have worked to get a faster time." Mum said as she moved away to get the dinner out of the oven.

"What's for dinner?" Willow said, thinking it was best to change the subject before Mum thought to ask why she was having a bad day.

"Hana's homemade lasagne with garlic bread and a side salad. I bet your hungry aren't you? Oh, and after dinner, can you remember to rinse your swimming costume and put it with your towel on the clothes line to dry?" Mum asked.

"Will do."

Hana was an excellent cook and Willow, despite her mood, wolfed down dinner, enjoying it immensely. The conversation over dinner included the usual daily things, but, thankfully, not one mention of the coming Handfasting.

Once dinner was finished and the pots were washed and put away, Willow rinsed her costume in the sink and hung it, and her towel, out on the line in their small back garden before making the excuse of having homework to do and went up to her room.

An hour later, Willow had completed her small amount of homework and was laid on her bed reading when her mum arrived with a mug in her hand.

'I thought you might like a hot chocolate, I know it cheers you up." She said as she placed the steaming mug on the bedside table and sat down on the edge of the bed. She seemed a bit edgy, almost nervous about something. "You seem quiet, is there anything bothering you?" She asked.

"No." Willow lied and didn't look up from her book. She hated lying, but her Mum just wouldn't understand.

"Well, if there is, you know you can talk to me about anything, don't you?" Mum said as she brushed her long brown hair behind her ear.

"I know, mum." She put her book down on her leg, "Thanks for the hot chocy."

"Your welcome, Will." Her Mum said with a smile and left Willow's room.

The next day, Willow spoke to Coach Ruby who agreed to do a retest after the end of school. Later, Willow stood by the pool, waiting until everyone from the last swimming class had left. She forced her problems at home out of her mind and determinedly dived into the pool to begin the retest. Before she knew it she was reaching the end of the four qualifying laps and quickly looked at the clock.

She had done it.

She had completed the lengths within the required time to make the team.

"Congratulations and welcome to the team, Willow!" Coach Ruby, the tall, thin, middle-aged lady said as she smiled down into the pool at Willow. "I knew you could do it."

"Thank you." Willow said as she heaved herself out of the water and grabbed her towel. She was so pleased with herself, not only had she made the team, but she had swum her best time, ever. For a while the pleasure and excitement of making the team dimmed her other problems and Willow smiled happily.

"See you at the team practice tomorrow, and remember, we have an in-team competition next week." Coach Ruby smiled as she began to tidy the pool before closing it for the night.

Rowan was waiting for her friend in the changing room and looked up, hopefully, as Willow entered.

"Well?" She asked.

"I'm on the team!" Willow said proudly.

"Oh, that's great. Well done." Rowan grinned, jumped up and hugged Willow enthusiastically.

"Thanks." Willow hugged her back and smiled.

"You know we have a team competition on Saturday, right? Coach says it to see who can get the best times in all the different strokes, then she'll know where to place us when we have competitions with other schools."

"Yes, she said. You'd better get some practise in, I might beat you." Willow said only half jokingly.

"It doesn't matter who wins, we both get be on the team." Rowan grinned, happy to be able to spend more time with her best friend and share the fun of being in the team. Rowan pulled out a chocolate bar and offered Willow a piece.

"Thanks. You know, my Mum says this will give you spots." Willow said holding up the chocolate before quickly popping it in her mouth and chewing it blissfully.

"So they say. Don't care. Swimming makes me very hungry." Rowan said as she too ate a piece.

"You're always hungry." Willow said.

Rowan nodded, "True. I am." She laughed. "Well, this time it's a celebration chocolate." She said and winked at Willow.

Laughing, the girls changed and heading home together. The only lived a couple of doors away from each other and they usually walked to school and back home again together.

The next week passed by quickly. Willow got in as much swimming practice as she could, which kept her mind busy from the happenings at home. Plans for the Handfasting were going on in earnest as May 1st, Beltane, was rapidly approaching, it was only a week away. Hana and April, Willow's Mum, were making their own Handfasting outfits. April was making the Blessing Cake and Hana was in charge of creating the invitations, which would be hand delivered by Willow.

Willow looked down on the kitchen table at the pile of invitation envelopes and homemade invitations that Hana was sat gluing. "Isn't it a bit late to give out invitations? People won't be able to come." She said, secretly hoping they couldn't, then it would just be them at the Handfasting and no one would know.

"That's been solved, thanks to Elder Daisy. Being the Mistress of Women's Mysteries she was to lead the ritual on Beltane, it being a fertility ritual and all, she offered to incorporate our Handfasting into the ritual. So we know everyone will be there." Mum said.

"The invites are mainly for the party afterwards." Hana said.

"It'll be great to celebrate our Handfasting and Beltane with everyone we know. Won't it be lovely?" Mum said.

Before Willow could think of a suitable reply, her Mum had put a pile of folded washing in her hands.

"Here, be a love and put these away for me. I have a billion things to do."

"Okay." Willow said, happy for a reason to escape the conversation.

She walked out of the kitchen with her arms full of washing just in time to hear Hana say, "These invites should be dry in the morning. They can be delivered tomorrow, maybe when Willow gets back from her competition. Do you think she will mind delivering them?" She asked.

"No, I'm sure she's glad to help." Mum said.

Willow scowled, she was glad she couldn't be seen as she went upstairs. She was suddenly very angry. How would they know if she minded? No one ever asked her.

She did indeed mind.

Very much.

The following day, Saturday, was to be a busy one for Willow. In the morning, Mum was taking her to the train station to pick up Marsh, Willow's older brother, as he was on holiday from college for the next two weeks. They were then stopping by Elder Heather's house to choose the flowering herbs that were to be used as the Handfasting flowers, then it was back home and lunch.

Mid afternoon, there was the swim team competition and then the final fitting of Willow's bridesmaid's dress and then Willow was to deliver the invitations. A task she really wasn't looking forward to, it would be the time that everyone would know. That really frightened Willow, what would they all think? How would she be able to face anyone at school afterwards?

The only good thing was, she didn't have time to deliver the invites before the competition. If she'd had to, Willow had decided to fake being sick just to not go and not have to see everyone looking at her when they all knew the truth.

Willow stood on the platform waiting for Marsh's train, luckily it was running a bit late, as were they. Mum had sent her in to find Marsh while she parked the car.

At last the train arrived, and Marsh stepped off it carrying his backpack. He was tall and dark haired like their Dad. He looked like him too, very handsome with large brown eyes and long lashes. Even though she was happy to see her brother, seeing him made Willow miss her Dad more. She was sad that her Dad never phoned anymore, nor did he ask for her to come and visit him and his new family.

"Hey squirt." Marsh said as he hugged her, "Where's Mum?"

"Just parking the car, we got here late." Willow said.

"Good job my train was late." He grinned, "Mum says you got on the swim team, congrats Sis."

"Thanks. We've got a competition this afternoon, are you going to come and watch?" Willow said.

"Sure thing, wouldn't miss it. Are you gonna win?"

"Of course." Willow smiled up at Marsh. She had missed him and she'd forgotten how much fun he was.

"Marsh, sorry I'm late. Did you have a good journey?" Mum said as she arrived out of breath.

"Yup, food is still bad on the trains though. When's lunch? I'm starving." He said winking at Willow.

The next few hours were so busy, they became a blur to Willow.

At last she stood in the changing room with the rest of the team, waiting for the coach to say they could go out into the pool area. From where she stood she could hear that the pool's stands were full, the sound echoed around the pool building and sounded like there were hundreds of people. Butterflies crash-dived in her stomach and her mouth became dry with nerves, it didn't help that she had awoken that morning with a sore throat.

"When we get out there, I want you to all line up against the wall on the right and come to the start positions when I call your names." Coach Ruby said, "Right, let's go."

Suddenly, Willow was no longer nervous, excitement took over as she walked out to the pool and her first official match in the team.

The stands were full of family and friends of all the team members, lots of the school teachers were there, as were the friends and family of the boys swim team who were also having a similar competition. The races would be one for the girls and then one for the boys in each stroke, this allowed a short rest for those swimmers who were entered into more than one discipline. There would be no races with boys against girls, this was not a test of 'who is the stronger sex' but rather who is the best, in each team, for the individual strokes for the inter-school races.

Willow had been entered in two races, the Front and Back Crawl, the same ones Rowan and two other girls had been entered in. The race for the Back Crawl would come after the Breaststroke race, which was just about to start.

Coach Ruby called out the names of the competitors for the first race. The crowd cheered as the swimmers took their places and continued to cheer them as the race began.

Willow watched as the swimmers did their best and really pushed themselves. She glanced around at the crowd and spotted her Mum with Marsh and Hana sitting on the third row. They weren't watching her but were cheering as the first girl's race quickly drew to an end.

The competitors got out of the pool and Coach Bay, the male counterpart to Coach Ruby, called his first competitors. Willow sat on a bench and tried patiently to wait her turn by watching the boys battle it out. Four lengths later and it was all over, the boys congratulated the winner as he got out of the pool.

Before long Willow heard her name being called, she nervously walked forward and stood with Rowan and the other two girls in front of the swim lanes. She stole a quick glance at her family, they were stood cheering and waving. It made Willow blush and she looked down trying to concentrate. The girls jumped in and got into position for the start of the Back Crawl and before Willow knew it, she was off racing against the other girls.

One of the others girls quickly took the lead and was quite a bit ahead at the first turn, but by the second she had begun to tire having shot off too fast. This left Rowan in the lead and, as they turned into the last length, with Willow a body's length behind her. Willow pushed and pushed herself until they were almost head to head, finally Rowan gave one final push and just won by a few inches. The crowd roared at such a tight race.

Gasping, the girls hugged each other. Willow happily congratulated her best friend, knowing she had done all she could, but Rowan was stronger in the Back Crawl than she was. The girls climbed out to make way for the boys' next race. When Willow sat back on the bench she looked over at her Mum again who was waving at her from the stands. Willow quickly waved and went back to watching the boys' race.

Finally, it was time for Willow's last race, the Front Crawl. The four girls took their positions at the edge of the pool and as soon as the beeper sounded they were off in one fast and smooth splash. Willow is stronger in the Front Crawl than the Back Crawl and immediately she was neck and neck with Rowan who had broken out in an early lead.

As they turned into the last lap, Willow began to edge into the front, she was just a few inches ahead of Rowan and gave one final push as the end of the race drew nearer. Willow reached the finishing line half a body length in front of Rowan.

She had done it.

She had won the race.

The crowd cheered as Willow climbed out of the pool, Rowan leapt out just as quickly and congratulated her. Willow's smile was huge as she waved to her family who were on their feet applauding. Her mum and Hana looked so happy together as the hugged each other and cheered.

Willow looked away, pleased with herself but self conscious of her two Mums and hoped none of her friends had been watching her family. A great loneliness washed over Willow, even though her friends and family surrounded her. She knew she was on her own, with no one to trust or confide in. There was no way to escape back to the changing rooms yet as the medals were to be awarded and the first and second team placements for each discipline were not to be announced until after the last race.

Willow sat down again, upon the wooden bench at the edge of the pool with the other team members and watched half heartedly as the race for the first and second positions in the Butterfly began. All Willow wanted to do was run to Grandmother Willow and hide behind her branches.

Finally, all the races were over and Coach Ruby and Coach Bay jointly congratulated everyone on their efforts. They then went on to announce the joint teams for each of the disciplines, two girls and two boys for each stroke. As each of the names we called the team member went up to collect their discipline awards, which were small sea stones engraved with the symbol for each stroke.

Willow was called up as the second for the Back Crawl and the first for the Front Crawl. As she walked towards the Coaches, Willow could feel her face turning red, she could feel the eyes of everyone in the building looking at her. It made her skin prickle and she felt awkward. She concentrated hard on the floor, hoping she wouldn't trip. She quickly took the sea stone and thanked the Coaches when they said she had done well. Willow peaked up at her family, just for a second, before concentrating back on the ground. In that brief flash, she saw her mum and Hana exchange a quick kiss on the lips and then hugged her brother as they cheered and clapped.

Willow was mortified and blushed even more. Didn't they know that all her friends were here? She wanted to scream at them, but knew she couldn't as that would bring even more attention to them.

At last, Willow could escape the pool and the hundreds of eyes and she rushed into the changing room in a desperate need to get away. Sadly, she couldn't escape entirely as she had to return home with her family and deliver the invitations.

"Well done, Will." Her Mum said, as she squeezed her in a big hug the second Willow emerged from the changing rooms.

"Congratulations." Hana said with a big smile.

"Well done, Squirt." Marsh said as he ruffled her wet hair.

"Thanks." Willow and forced a smile on her face hoping it looked convincing.

"I thought we would go to Iris's Café and have some cake and tea to celebrate, what do you think Willow?" Mum said as they all walked out of the school.

"Hmmm...sounds good, can I have a chocolate éclair?" Willow asked.

"Of course, you can have anything you like. It's your celebration tea, after all." Mum said.

Willow enjoyed the éclair and homemade lemonade but her mind kept coming back to what she was about to do.

The invitations.

The entire village would know and she would be the odd one out forever.

Willow just wanted to run away and hide.

Before long Willow found herself walking up an assortment of gravelled, bricked and stone pathways, which led to the many doors and letterboxes of those invited to the Handfasting celebration at the village hall after the ritual. As she posted each one, her sadness grew. She knew nothing would ever be the same again.

On one such delivery, she came across Blossom, her friend Yew's lovely Grandmother.

"Hello dearie, are you looking for Yew? I think she is in the back garden mending a puncture on her bike." Blossom said as she stood up from where she was kneeling weeding the flowerbed. She was a small round woman with long white hair that was tied back in a ponytail. She stretched her back as she straightened up.

"Err...no. I was just delivering this." Willow said as she offered Blossom the small envelope.

"Oh? What is it?" Blossom said and quickly ripped it open.

Willow had the sudden urge to run away. She didn't want Blossom to read it while she was there.

Blossom scanned the invite quickly as Willow started to back away.

"I have to go..." Willow mumbled as she fled back down the path and ran up the street, past all the houses she was supposed to deliver to.

Willow found herself out of breath and standing in the centre of the village, opposite the village green and next to the stone statue of Sage Featherstone, the founder of the village of Brew. She lent on the statue catching her breath reading the simple bronze plaque. 'Sage Featherstone, 1786 – 1837.' Under his name was a quote from him. 'Thy can not change who thy is, nor others, but thy can gather others of same around thee.' Founder of Brew, 1813.

"At least you found people you could talk to." Willow said grumpily, just as the sky burst open and a heavy rain began to fall. She clutched the cloth bag with the invites in close to her side and decided to run down the path by the river and wait out the rainstorm under the protective branches of Grandmother Willow.

By the time Willow had made cover, she was dripping like a wet rat, her hair was plastered to her head and her t-shirt and jeans clung to her uncomfortably. Unfortunately, the cloth bag was also soaked through and she could see the ink bleeding through the soggy envelopes of the last of the invites. There were about twenty left and they were all ruined. The sight of the wet envelopes, after all the ups and downs of the day, just made Willow burst into tears. She sat heavily on the stone near the trunk of Grandmother Willow and sobbed her heart out.

Eventually, the tears stopped and she sat there hiccupping, feeling totally at a loss. Everything in her life was such a mixture of good and bad that she just didn't know what to do next. Yes, she had gotten onto the swim team and won a first in the Front Crawl, but how could she stay on the team now? Knowing that everyone will be opening their invites and will treat her differently. She didn't want to be different, she didn't want to stand out and not be like everyone else and most importantly she wished she had someone to talk to about it.

She dreaded going home now that the last of the invites were ruined, she knew she would have to explain why she ran with them instead of delivery them and then she would have to admit why she didn't want two mums. She buried her face in her hands and began to cry again.

The evening was drawing in and it began to get chilly, but still Willow sat in her special place within the boughs of the great weeping willow tree. The light was beginning to fade and it was growing dim within the shelter of the tree. She was very late home and she knew she would get into trouble for that too, but she just couldn't face anyone at the minute.

"Why, can't you talk to me Grandmother Willow? Tell me what to do. Please." Willow begged the branches. Again, no answer came except the rustling of the leaves.

"Willow? Are you in there?" The voice demanded as the branches suddenly swished back and Marsh stepped into the hidden depths of the tree. "There you are! You've had us all worried to death!" Marsh said angrily, but then he saw Willows tears stained face and puffy eyes and quickly sat down on the stone to hug her. "What's wrong? What happened? Are you okay?" He said.

"Yes...no." She didn't look up at him, "I got caught in the rain, the invites are ruined and it's all my fault."

"How is it your fault? You didn't make it rain. I'm sure they aren't completely ruined. Anyway, what are you doing here? Mum's was on the verge of calling the police until I said I'd come and look for you. You should have been home hours ago."

"No...I...I stopped delivering them and they got wet, if I had finished posting them..."

"Why did you stop delivering them, Will?" He said.

"B...because I don't want people to know." Willow said as she started to cry again.

"Hey, it's okay. Everything's okay, I'm sure Hana can make up a few more invites, no problem." He said helpfully.

Willow suddenly stood up as a deep rage took over her, "I don't mean the invites." She shouted, "I meant the Handfasting, I don't want anyone to know about that." She stalked to the edge of the branches and fiddled with some of the wet leaves.

"Wait, what? Why don't you want people to know about the Handfasting?" He said, surprised by the sudden outburst.

"I don't want to be different from everyone else. I don't want two mums. I don't want everyone to laugh at me and..." Willow stopped and turned to look at her brother. "I want a normal family." She said flatly.

Marsh stood and moved closer to his sister, "You like Hana don't you?"

"Yes, she's nice."

"And you like how happy Hana makes mum, right?"

"Yes."

He placed his hand on Willows arm, "Then surely you understand that they want to be together and live together?"

"Yes."

"Then...all that's bothering you is what others think?" He looked surprised.

"I guess."

Marsh took her hand and led her back to the stone where they both sat down again in the twilight. "Look, all through life there will be people who disapprove of anything you do. It's just how some people are, but are you going to let their way of thinking effect what and how you do things? You need to rely upon yourself and do what is right for you not them. Isn't this life a little short for us to live it by other people's opinions?"

"I never thought of it that way." Willow said as she wiped her nose and sat thinking. "But what about my friends, what if they don't want to be my friends anymore?" She looked at him with panic in her eyes.

"If they don't then they weren't true friends to start with, were they?"

"Hmm..." Willow said.

"Why didn't you ring me and tell me you were feeling like this?" He said.

"You're too busy at college and...I...I thought you would think I was being silly." She said and blushed.

"I'm never too busy to talk to you, Squirt. You know that. And for the record, I wouldn't have thought you were being silly. Have you talked to anyone else?"

"No. I didn't want anyone to know and then when they wanted me to delivery the invites, I realised everyone would know at once." Willow sniffed, "Blossom, Yew's Grandmother, opened her invite in front of me and I just couldn't wait to see her face and so I ran and then it rained, so I came here." She wiped her nose, "I hated not having anyone to talk to. I've been so lonely."

Marsh hugged her close, "It's okay, Will. Everything will be okay." He pulled out his phone and rang home telling their mum that he had found Willow safe.

They then sat hugging for a long time until Willows hiccups from crying had subsided and she felt like talking again.

Willow's stomach rumbled and she realised that she had also missed dinner, "Is mum very angry with me?" She said as she looked up at Marsh.

"Not angry, just worried. We'd best get home and get that beast inside you fed." He winked at her, "I think the rain's stopped now." He stood and checked outside. "Yup, it has. Let's get going before it starts again." He grinned.

Willow stood to follow her brother, she felt different somehow, lighter even. Being able to talk to Marsh and tell him everything that had been bothering her, had made her feel better somehow.

"Thanks..." she said, "for everything."

"It's what big brothers are for, don't you know?" He winked at her as they began to walk down the path that lead back home, both of them trying to avoid the rain puddles in the growing darkness.

As they walked up the road to their house, Willow began to get worried. "You won't tell mum, will you?"

"About which bit? The invites or how you have been feeling?"

"About how I've been feeling." Willow said.

"I won't if you don't want me to, but I think she needs to know about it, though."

"I'll tell her after the Handfasting, I don't want to ruin it for her. Promise you won't?"

"I promise, but make sure you do." He said, "And I'm sure it won't ruin it for her, though. She would be happy if she thought you could talk to her about it."

They had reached the front door just as their mum opened it and hugged Willow very tightly with relief.

Once the initial relief was over and Willow was sat at the table eating her reheated dinner, she explained that the rain had ruined the invites that she had not yet posted and that she had sheltered from the storm under the weeping willow. Her mum was so relieved to have her back safely, she didn't mind about the invites at all and Hana began to make replacements at once so they could be delivered the following day.

As it was, Willow didn't have to deliver them, Marsh had done it. Willow had awoken with a terrible head cold and spent most of the day in bed. Luckily, the next week was a school holiday so Willow could stay warm and at home and let the cold virus take its course. However, the nearer Saturday and the Handfasting got, the more nervous Willow became. It would be the first time she had seen anyone since the news of the Handfasting had gone out.

Beltane, like all festival days and celebrations, was to be held on the Goddess Mound, a hillock that was the shaped of a pregnant tummy. On top of the mound were the ancient thirteen stones of the circle of Brew and the village of Brew's altar to the God and Goddess.

The first of May, which is Beltane and the Handfasting day, had started early with the ladies of the village going out and collecting the morning dew to wash their faces with, a tradition that had been passed down through the generations of villagers. Willow hadn't gone this year as she still had a lingering cough from the cold virus and her mum thought it was wise not to get her cold and damp.

Finally, the time for the Handfasting had come and Willow stood with her mum, Hana and Marsh at the base of the Goddess mound looking up towards the Goddess Mound. They were the last to go up, as was traditional for the Handfasting party. The mound had been decorated with flowers and torches and the entire village lined the path to the top. Once the Handfasting party was at the top, the villagers would fill in around them and the ritual would begin.

April and Hana held hands and smiled at each other, both were dressed in long deep green dresses with yellow Celtic embroidery at the sleeves and hems. They both had flowers and herbs in their hair. With a final hand squeeze, they began the walk up the winding path of the mound past the cheering villagers. Willow kept her head down, not making eye contact with anyone and clung to Marsh's arm that he had offered her to walk up the hill.

The exertion made Willow cough by the time they had made it to the top, but still she did not look around. At last everyone was in position within the circle of stones and the villagers had gathering around the outside of the stones.

Elder Daisy, Mistress of Women's Mysteries and Co-Leader of the Elders of Brew, began the welcome and the traditional Beltane Blessing. Willow watched as Elder Daisy spoke, the words washing over her, her mind full of what others might be thinking at this moment.

Small and curvy, with one of those faces that never stopped smiling, Elder Daisy had a very gentle, but authorative voice. She had shoulder length thick hair, which was wavy and completely silver. Her words finally cut in through Willows distracted thoughts.

"Today, we are here to celebrate the blessings of Beltane and also the blessing of a union, that of the Handfasting of April and Hana. Please can the Handfasting party step forward?" Elder Daisy said.

With a lurch in her stomach, Willow stepped a few paces forward with her family and she watched as Elder Daisy made the Blessings of the God and Goddess over her mum and Hana. The deep green ribbon, embroidered with the same Celtic design as their dresses, was bound about their wrists and hands

as a symbol of their lives being bound together, they exchanged vows and were at last being given the final blessing by
Elder Daisy. She came to the end of the Blessing but before she
announced the newly Handfasted couple to the villagers as was
usual at this part of the ritual, she paused.

April and Hana looked at the Elder expectantly as did all
the villagers, wondering why she had paused. Elder Daisy
briefly nodded and stepped back a couple of spaces.

Willow walked forward and stood in the Elder's place.

She looked around at everyone, they all had the same surprised and expectant look on their faces.

Her stomach exploded with nervous butterflies, but she was
determined to do this. Willow coughed once and again nervously. "Before Elder Daisy finished I..." Willow cleared her
throat, licked her dry lips and took and deep breath. She said
louder this time, "Before Elder Daisy announced this Handfasting as complete, I asked if I could say something too."

Marsh's eyebrows rose almost to his hairline in surprise.

April, Willow's mum and Hana exchanged looks and then
looked back at Willow, also surprised. Their happiness was
shining through their faces. Willow had never seen them both
look so happy and she was glad that she had delayed telling her
mum how she felt. All the worry instantly melted away in that
one moment as her mind became very clear.

She realised, at long last, that it didn't matter what the others thought.

"We all know that this village was founded by Sage Featherstone because he wanted to live with people like him, Pagans
and nature lovers and this has been so for everyone who has
lived here since he built the town in...1813, I think it was." Willows eyes flicked to her brother.

Marsh nodded, grinning.

"I am proud of my mum for doing what truly makes her happy and being Handfasted to Hana has made her very happy. I can see it." Willow swallowed hard. Her eyes brimmed with happy tears as did her mum's.

"I understand now that you must do what makes you happy in life, even if others don't approve or don't agree with you. You must rely on yourself to create your own happiness, as long as you are not hurting anyone or the earth and the animals. Like someone told me recently, why let others tell you how to be happy? I know now that it's okay to be different, to have two mums when others don't. I understand that everyone's version of a family is different, but no matter how it's different, it's still a family. I wanted to say that and welcome Hana to my family, I'm proud to have her as my second mum." Willow eyes overflowed with happy tears that ran down her face.

Elder Daisy quickly stepped forward and put her arm around Willow "With the Blessings of the Elders and the villagers of Brew, I now pronounce April and Hana Handfasted."

A huge cheer went up as April and Hana quickly kissed to seal the Blessing and Elder Daisy whispered in Willows ear "Well said, Willow, well said."

Marsh then whisked Willow up in a brotherly hug and said in her ear, "You do realise that all of Brew already knew, don't you? Mum and Hana have been openly dating and planning this Handfasting, the entire village already knew and happily accepts it. Mum explained it to me this morning, just before we left."

A flood of joy overwhelmed Willow, "Really? I had no idea."

"You see, you should talk to people more." He grinned, "You know, you were never alone, you just had to reach out." And before Willow could speak another word she was smothered buy a group hug from all the members of her new family.

Ivy the Stubborn Witch

An Introduction to Ivy

For many years, each person in Brew has been named after things in Nature and Ivy is no exception.

The Ivy plant is able to thrive and grow in almost all environments, it is extremely strong and is very difficult to destroy. Its stalks grow in what appears a helix and therefore represents the growing spiral of self-enlightenment that was sacred to the Celts. It also symbolizes the soul and its journeys both inner and outer on its search for nourishment.

Ivy, who is named after the plant, is eleven years old, tall and slim, she has long dark hair and brilliant green eyes, which would turn pale green when she cries. Her friends think that she is fun but she can be very stubborn too.

Ivy enjoys most of the seasons but her least favourite is summer. She hates it. She hates being hot and sticky, hates having to wear sunscreen and hats, and most of all, hates it because her cousin, Honey, comes to stay with her family for a month every summer and she has to share her bedroom.

Our tale begins in the height of summer and just a few days before the Summer Solstice, otherwise known as Litha. The Summer Solstice is the time when the day is at its longest and the sun is celebrated.

Ivy the Stubborn Witch

Ivy looked down at today's page in her diary.

It said one word: HONEY.

The capital letters stood out on the otherwise blank page and were underlined, vigorously, in red pen.

She sighed deeply, slammed the dairy shut and threw it in her desk drawer. Ivy stared at the drawer for a few moments, stood up from her desk chair and flopped down on the window cushion, looking out at the dark brooding clouds overhead.

"Ivy? Is your room ready? Honey will be here in about twenty minutes. Your dad's just left for the station." Ivy's mum, Cherry, called up the stairs.

"Yes, mum."

Ivy looked around her room. It was a little tidier than usual, although she was quite a tidy person anyway but mum had insisted it was 'cleaned up' for Honey's visit.

"It's just not fair." Ivy said to herself. Why should she share her room every year, for a whole month, with her spoilt cousin? Why couldn't Honey sleep on the sofa bed in dad's office? Surely it was better than the camp cot in her room, she thought.

Ivy had wanted to go to the river today, she loved how summer storms made the water look dark and mysterious and she loved to run her fingers along the cold stonework of the old bridge. Plus everyone else was going to the river to watch the storm roll over the hills. She wanted to be there and dance in the warm rain as the other girls would. But no, she wasn't allowed to. She had to stay home to 'welcome' Honey, just as her mum had told her and help her to feel 'at home'. Feel at home? How could she possibly feel at home in our small cottage when she lives in a mansion, in the city, with servants, tutors and rich friends?

It had not always been this way.

Many years ago when the cousins were smaller, Ivy and Honey had played happily together and the summer visits had always flown by. Things changed two years ago when Honey's parents had brought in a private tutor and Honey no longer attended public school. At this time, Honey became withdrawn and less talkative, the girls had simply drifted apart. Now, they seemed to be from different universes, never mind worlds.

With a heavy sigh, Ivy grabbed her most loved, also the most torn and tattered book from her bedside table, Pride and Prejudice. Sitting back on her window seat, she tried to lose herself in the old tale of manners, morals and marriages in 19th century England. Unfortunately, it wasn't long before the sound of Honey's high-pitched nervous laughter distracted Ivy and instantly annoyed her. 'I guess the plight of Miss Bennett and Mr Darcy would have to wait.' She said, disappointedly, to nobody but herself.

Within moments, Ivy could hear her mum calling her downstairs to greet their guest. She knew she had no choice but to do as she was asked and put up with her cousin for four long, and very tedious, weeks.

Slowly she walked to the top of the staircase, wishing this was the day that Honey was leaving, not arriving. Looking down she saw the usual sight of her mum making a fuss over Honey with lots of hugs and 'How you have grown.' and 'You do look like your mother, how is my dear sister, Juniper?' Ivy groaned, it was like watching an old movie that you had 'grown out of' but still knew all the words to.

Honey was as beautiful as ever, matching her name in looks and personality. She had long golden hair, perfect skin, pale brown eyes and a warm friendly outlook on life. She was dressed in the latest fashions from the most expensive shops.

Ivy watched as Honey smiled brightly and hugged Ivy's mum warmly. She was just too sweet and sickly to be true. Gritting her teeth and trying not to think about her second hand clothes, Ivy fixed her best smile on her face just as Honey looked up and smiled shyly at her.

"Ivy, come and help Honey carry her bags upstairs, will you?" Mum said, "I'll put the kettle on, fancy a cup of tea, Honey?"

"Oh, yes please. That would be great." Honey said and smiled at her favourite Aunt. She began to climb up stairs carrying her two large designer bags, struggling with each and every step.

"Oh...come here." Ivy ran down a few steps and grabbed one of the bags, whirled round and headed for her bedroom, without another word. She dumped the heavy bag on the camp bed, picked up her book quickly, to avoid any conversation, and sat back in her favourite spot at the window before Honey had even entered the room.

"It's...nice to see you again, cousin." Honey said quietly as she placed her bag on the bed, looked round the small bedroom and began unzipping the bags.

"Hmmm..." Ivy said without looking up and continued to read. She could hear Honey hanging clothes in the wardrobe and placing t-shirts and other clothes in the spare chest of drawers. She tried hard to ignore the sounds.

The extended silence was becoming more and more awkward.

"What are you reading? What ever it is, it looks like you are enjoying it." Honey said.

Ivy didn't answer, she just held up the cover of the book in Honey's general direction and then went back to reading it.

"Ah...yes. An excellent book, my tutor always says that it...."

Ivy interrupted her with a loud sigh and continued to look at her book.

"I...I'm sorry. I didn't mean to disturb you." Honey paused for a moment, obviously unsure of what to do next. "I'll go and see if Aunt Cherry has poured the tea." Honey said quietly and, with one last glance at Ivy, left the room.

The next few days were very frustrating for both Ivy and Honey. It rained constantly and they were stuck indoors, worst of all, they were stuck indoors together. Each of them had books in hand and sat in opposite ends of the house reading them. They avoided spending time together with every ounce of their beings, unless they had to be in the same room at mealtimes or when Ivy's mum dragged them together to do something as a family. These times were always very strained with stilted conversations.

Usually, when the weather was nice, they could do as they had done for the last two years and gone out during the day, with one going one way and the other going in the opposite direction. They had always managed to keep themselves occupied and had met up just around the corner from Ivy's house, to make it look like they had spent the day together. However, this was not possible when it rained and it made them both even more miserable.

The rain finally let up the following morning but everything outside was too sodden and muddy to do anything really interesting and, seeing that it was Saturday and Ivy's dad, Heath, was home, Ivy's mum decided they would play board games together after lunch. Ivy was not looking forward to it. It's so difficult to communicate with someone you have nothing in common with and whom you didn't want in your bedroom, but what choice did she have?

Mum had everyone organized; she had found the Backgammon and Chess games from the cupboard. Dad had got out his Tafl game and challenged mum to a game, leaving Honey and Ivy to play one of the two remaining games.

"Which do you want to play?" Ivy said and sighed quietly.

"I don't mind...." Honey said.

"Right then." Ivy grabbed the Backgammon and started setting it up without another glance at Honey.

They played in absolute silence, which was only broken by mum and dad talking and laughing over their game.

Ivy wished the game would be over quickly so she could return to her reading or computer and, because she had been made to play, she did so gracelessly. Every time it was her turn she shook the dice quickly and stomped her pieces on the board loudly.

Honey played quietly.

The moment the game was finished Ivy stood up.

"I'm going to lie down, I have a headache." She said.

"Oh, alright love." Said her mum, "Do you need anything?"

"No, I think it is just the change of weather, I will be okay. Thanks." Ivy said and made her way upstairs to her bedroom. She hadn't lied, exactly, she did have a bit of a headache but not as bad as she had implied, she just couldn't stand having to be with Honey for much longer even though Honey had been very quiet. The more Ivy thought about how she behaved around Honey, the more angry she became.

Ivy closed the door and, knowing she wouldn't be disturbed for an hour or so, decided to start Little Women, her summer reading project for English class, having finished Pride and Prejudice that morning. She could easily stash it under the bed if someone came in to check on her.

Much later that afternoon, mum walked into Ivy's room carrying a pile of clothes, "How is the headache?" She said.

"It's gone, I guess it wasn't as bad as I thought." Ivy said, a little embarrassed at her slight deception.

"Glad to hear it." Mum said as she moved across the room, "So what's going on with you and Honey?" She said.

"Nothing, why?" Ivy said.

Mum started placing the clothes in Ivy's dresser, "Have you fallen out? You have hardly said a word to each other since she has been here.' Mum said as she finished putting the clothes away and sat on the end of Ivy's bed by her feet.

"No." Ivy avoided her eyes. Impatiently she got up, walked over to the window and sat on the window seat. She stared out of the window into the ever-darkening afternoon.

"Ivy, what's going on?" Mum said.

"Nothing."

"I think something is. You know how much Honey loves coming here."

"Does she? She doesn't seem to."

"Yes, she does. She begs her parents not to be placed in a summer school every year just so she can come here. She is so very happy around your father and I, which makes me wonder why she isn't around you. Why is that, do you think?"

"I don't know. Perhaps you should ask her." Ivy said sulkily.

"Listen, Ivy, please try harder to be nice to Honey while she is a guest in this house. She gets little enough of a family at-mosphere as it is at home. Will you try harder?" Mum said as she stood up and moved towards the door.

"Okay, Mum. I'll try...just for you." Ivy tried to smile but only managed a half smile that probably looked like a grimace.

"Good, all I ask is that you try your best, Ivy. That's all. She is a lovely young lady and you two used to be such good friends." Mum looked sad and left the room.

Ivy took a deep breath and blew it out noisily, then turned back to glare out the window. The twilight of early evening was making everything a slight purple colour and hard to see. Ivy sighed heavily, leaned over to switch on the lamp by her bed and tried to go back to her book but she just couldn't concentrate. Her mum's words kept swirling about in her mind. What had her mum meant when she said that Honey gets 'little enough of a family atmosphere at home'?

The following day, the sun finally revealed itself from behind the grey clouds and the temperature began to climb back up into the normal range for the middle of June. However, due to all the rain the day was humid and sticky. Cherry insisted that if both girls wanted to go out today they must wear sunscreen and hats as the temperature was expected to soar around lunchtime.

Honey didn't seem to mind and was happy to lather the cream on but Ivy hated it, she hated the sticky humid weather, the sunscreen and having to wear a silly hat. All these things put Ivy in a bad mood that was almost as dark as yesterday's storm clouds. Ivy didn't argue with her mother, she knew it was pointless, she just grumpily wore the hat and the cream until both girls were out of sight of the house and then she quickly removed her hat, stuffing it into her skirt pocket.

"Don't tell my mum. Okay?" Ivy said.

"Why should I? It's your head." Honey said.

"Yes, it is." Ivy said as she stalked off down a side lane, leaving Honey standing on her own.

Honey sighed and began to walk in the opposite direction. She was used to Ivy dumping her to escape and had already decided to spend the day down by the river with its cool breeze and shade. She had even brought along a book and some lunch. She was looking forward to a nice relaxing day.

Several hours later, Honey sat in the cool shade of a large willow, its branches and leaves gently moved by the warm breeze as they trailed in the water. She was happily watching a dragonfly flit from one plant to another, it's long thin body was a beautiful shade of iridescent blue, when suddenly she heard a scream and a huge splash.

Alarmed, Honey jumped up and looked around her, she could see nothing unusual down the river to her right but to her left there was a bend and she could not see round it. She quickly grabbed her bag and ran towards the bend, panicked and wondering if someone was hurt. As she turned the corner she saw Holly, Ivy's best friend, standing on the old stone bridge shouting to someone in the water. Honey rushed over to find Ivy swimming to the river's edge.

"What happened?" Honey said.

"We were walking on the wall of the old bridge when she just fell off." Holly said as she tried to reach for her friend. Holly was taller than Honey with long, dark brown hair, bright shiny blue eyes and a very slightly bent nose, which was the painful present from her younger brother last summer.

"I didn't 'just' fall off. I suddenly felt dizzy and slipped." Ivy said as she staggered to the bank and took Holly's hand to help her climb up it. She stood there absolutely soaked with water running in rivulets down her arms and legs. Her sandals and feet were covered in mud from the riverbank.

"Are you okay?" Asked Holly.

"Yeah, I'm fine. Got a big headache though." Ivy said.

"Did you hit your head?" Holly asked.

"No."

"You've got sunstroke because you didn't wear your hat." Honey said, "You should slowly drink some water and the headache will go."

"Thanks, Dr. Honey." Ivy said as she angrily grabbed the material of her skirt and began to wring out some of the water.

Holly passed Ivy a bottle of water from her backpack, "Honey is probably right, you know." She said.

"Oh, I'm sure she is." Ivy said with a sigh and slowly began to drink the water, "I'm off home to get changed, see you tomorrow." With that Ivy stormed off back towards home, her wet sandals squeaking with every step.

Honey had no choice but to say goodbye to Holly and follow Ivy home, they were supposed to be spending the day together after all.

Cherry looked up from beheading her rose bushes just in time to see Honey and, a very wet Ivy, walk through the garden gate.

"What happened to you?" She said, trying hard not to smile at her soaked daughter with a miserable face.

"We were messing around and I pushed Ivy into the river. It was stupid of me, I know, but we were having so much fun. I'm sorry, Aunt Cherry." Honey said before Ivy could say a word.

Both Ivy and her mum stared at Honey in disbelief. Honey had never done anything like this before. She had never lied for Ivy nor misbehaved whilst in Cherry and Heath's home.

"Well, then...I guess you had better help Ivy inside and help clean up after her too." Cherry said, not wanting to tell Honey off. After all, the girls had actually been having fun together and, luckily, no harm was done.

The girls quickly went inside, Honey grabbed a towel as Ivy took of her muddy, wet sandals.

"Why did you do that? Why did you tell my mum you pushed me in?" Ivy said.

"Because you would have got in trouble for not wearing your hat and getting sunstroke. How is the headache by the way?"

"Better thanks...and...thanks...for covering for me."

"You're welcome. Perhaps you should wear your hat next time though." Honey said as a shy smile spread across her face.

"Perhaps I will." Ivy said and headed upstairs for a warm shower and dry, clean clothes.

That evening, after a slightly less awkward dinner, Ivy found Honey in the bedroom sitting on the camp bed, writing in what looked like a diary. She was also mumbling to herself angrily. Ivy stood quietly behind her at the doorway, wondering if she should go in and disturb her but then she would have to talk to her or just turn round and come back later.

Honey suddenly burst into tears and sat sobbing over her writing.

Ivy was mortified.

Had she made Honey so miserable that she would sit here alone and sob? Ivy felt her cheeks redden in shame.

"Erm...are you okay?" Ivy said at last.

Honey jumped.

In one swift movement she had closed her book and twirled around. Her hand shot to her face and quickly wiped away her tears.

"Yes, I'm alright...sorry, did you want to be alone in here?" Honey said without looking directly at Ivy.

"No...well, yes...but...why were you crying?" Ivy realised she wanted to know if it was her fault or not, but thinking about her behaviour towards Honey made her blush again. Ivy stepped into the room, "You don't have to tell me...I just wanted to get my laptop, and I'll be out of your way in a minute." Ivy rushed across the room thoroughly embarrassed and grabbed her laptop off her desk accidentally knocking over her pen pot in her hurry. Pens shot in every direction and bounced off the desk like jumping beans.

"Oh damn it." Ivy said. She quickly placed the laptop back on the desk, crawled underneath and began picking up the pens and the many paper clips that had been hiding in the bottom of the pot.

Honey was there, instantly, helping to pick them up. She handed a handful of pens and paperclips back to Ivy and smiled shyly, her lovely complexion was all mottled with red blotches from crying and her eyes had turned a strange pale brown colour from the tears.

"Thanks." Ivy said as she took the pens and paper clips. "Are you sure you're okay?"

"Yes. I...I just hate...invading your room when you obviously don't want me here. I love coming to stay with your family. I even love the way you all do things together and are involved in...each others...lives." The words tumbled out and Honey blushed as silent tears ran down her face. She quickly looked away and went back to sit on the camp bed. "I'm sorry." She said as she cried quietly.

Ivy didn't know what to say as she placed the pens and paper clips back in their pot with a loud clatter. She felt very guilty for not making Honey feel more welcome than she had. "Don't cry...." Ivy handed her a tissue.

Honey gently wiped her eyes.

"Before I came, I asked your mum if I could use the sofa bed in your father's room instead of getting in your way but she said no because it would be nice for us both...if we shared the same room. I'm sorry, I tried not to be in your way but I couldn't change her mind."

"Oh...you're not in my way...not really. I'm sorry too, I've not been very welcoming to you. Is that why you are crying?"

"Yes and no. Although, I love coming here...it always makes me sad too. Aunt Cherry and Uncle Heath are great. You are very lucky." Honey tried to smile.

"Thanks...your parents are great too." Ivy smiled encouragingly.

"Hmm...sometimes I wish I had yours."

"Why?" Ivy said as she sat down next to Honey on the camp bed.

"My parents are far too busy to do anything with me. Father is always working or travelling abroad and mother runs her Gallery and travels too. I usually get left with Sophie, my nanny who treats me like a four year old or Mr. Alexander, my tutor, who makes me study...even during the holidays." Honey blew her nose and wiped the last of her tears away. "The only fun I have is coming here once a year and it's getting harder and harder to persuade my parents that I prefer it here rather than going to that stupid summer camp for young ladies." She said.

"What camp?" Ivy asked.

"Oh it's horrid, I tried it last year...do you remember that I arrived a few days late last year? That was because my parents had sent me to the camp but I hated it. They make you study how to be a socially correct young lady by teaching you things like how to fold napkins and arrange flowers. It's like something from my history lessons and the place is full of mean girls. I hated every second. I got Sophie to bring me home after the first week then we rang mother in Italy and persuaded her that I should come here instead."

"Wow! I never knew anything about the camp. I knew your parents travel a lot, but not that much. Why don't you go with them? At least you would see the world?" Ivy said.

"I asked once, they didn't seem very interested, they said that if I did Sophie and Mr. Alexander would have to come to, to take care of me. So I said no because it was no different than being at home." Honey sighed sadly.

Ivy looked at her and saw, for the first time, just how truly sad she was. A sudden thought came to her and it even surprised her as she said it out loud. "Well, I guess we should make the most of your time with us then, huh? Tomorrow is the eve of the Summer Solstice and we will all be at the Stones overnight to watch the sun come up. How would you like to watch it with my friends and I? Instead of staying with mum and dad, like you did last year?" Ivy said excitedly and reached out to touch Honey's hand. She was amazed that she felt the need to comfort and share things with her.

"Really? You mean that? I can spend some time with you and your friends?"

"Yes, really. I think we should do more things together on this visit because I don't like to see you so sad." Ivy said.

"Thank you." Honey said as she threw her arms around Ivy in a big hug.

Ivy gladly returned the hug and found that she was smiling. She felt happy for the first time during this visit.

Honey and Ivy sat huddled together in blankets as the chill of the early morning tried to seep into their bones.

They were surrounded by the entire village of Brew, who were sat inside the circle of thirteen stones. The stones stood majestically on the hillock known as the Goddess Mound, because of it similarity to a pregnant woman. Everyone had gathered together for the return of the sun on the Summer Solstice morning. It was traditional in Brew to greet the sun and then, after the ritual of thanks for its return, all the villagers would walk down to the village green, in the centre of the village, where a street party was set up with food, games and other entertainment.

Ivy loved this celebration of mid-summer and she was really enjoying it this year in the company of Honey. Over the last day Honey and Ivy had been reconnecting and having long talks about everything in their lives, from parents to friends, from favourite books to boys, from the food they hate to the places they most wanted to visit. They had regained their old friendship and remembered just how much fun it was to spend time together.

Honey and Ivy sat watching the sky lighten as the sun started to rise and gently warm the air. Even this early in the day, the moment the sun peeped over the horizon the chill was reduced and a faint warmth was felt by all.

The villagers' burst into cheers and clapping at the sight of the sun, a few started to sing a blessing song for its return and steadily everyone joined in. The two girls stood, still hugging each other within their blanket, and sang the song of blessing at the tops of their voices, smiles spreading on their happy faces.

The thirteen Elders of Brew, all dressed in golden robes, recited the ancient blessing of the sun and raised a drinking horn to toast the new day. They gave offerings to the Earth Mother and Father Sun for the harvest of the summer season. A cheer was raised, as many horns were passed around so that the villagers of Brew could toast the sun with mead, the golden liquid of the Gods.

The ritual part of the celebration came to an end as families picked up their blankets and chairs and began to make their way down the steep winding path of the Goddess Mound towards the village green and the breakfast party.

Honey and Ivy joined Ivy's friends as they walked down the spiral pathway of the mound.

"This is Ash, she moved here at the Spring Equinox. Ash this is Honey, my cousin." Ivy said, "And that is Rufus, the mad terrier."

"Hello." Ash said and smiled.

Ash was the same height as Honey but had very long blond hair and pale blue eyes.

"Hello, nice to meet you." Honey smiled and noticed that Ash had a small brown birthmark on her upper left cheek, shaped like a tiny cloud. Honey reached down to stroke Rufus, who was a wonderful golden coloured terrier, "Do you like living here, Ash?" She said.

"I love it. Wasn't sure I would fit in at first but everyone is so friendly and nice here, it's like one big happy family." Ash said as she smiled and walked beside Honey.

"Yes, I like that too...very much." Honey said.

Ivy drew back to walk beside Holly.

"I thought you didn't get along with your cousin anymore." Holly whispered to Ivy.

Ivy looked at her friend. "I didn't used to but we're getting on a lot better this time and I've noticed we like a lot of the same things. She is actually very nice." Ivy said.

"I know, I have always liked her. I couldn't understand why you two seemed to have forgotten that you are family and have fun whenever you're together." Holly said.

"Yeah, I don't know how we forgot that either. I guess I was being a bit stubborn with not wanting to share my bedroom." Ivy said.

"You? Stubborn? Never!" Holly said.

Ivy playful punched Holly on the arm and they both laughed.

"Watch it or I shall make you eat your own Strawberry cheesecake." Ivy said trying not to giggle, knowing full well that Holly's cheesecake was the best in the village.

"Hey, my cheesecake is yummy."

"I'll race you to the first bite then." Shouted Ivy as she ran between Honey and Ash in her rush to get away from Holly, making Rufus bark with excitement.

All the girls laughed and began to race down the rest of the path and along the lane to the village green where the villagers were busy uncovering the food and setting out the drinks.

Moon Scape, the local band, was warming up their instruments for the dancing. Around the green several games were being set up on the road, which circled it. Some teenagers were setting up a game of Skittles, which is very much like ten pin bowling but with old, and somewhat battered, wooden pins and balls. On the large grass verge outside the bakers and the post office, there was even a short game of Croquet being set up.

There were several tables covered in food. Each family had donated a dish or two to the feast, each dish was either shaped or related to the rising of the sun or made from summer produce. There were hard boiled eggs cut in half showing the sunny yolks, bread loaves shaped like the sun alongside the salads decorated with yellow flowers and bowls of fresh strawberries with cream. Everything was beautifully displayed and looked very tasty. There were also stalls of hot and cold drinks, all free in honour of the festival day.

The atmosphere was that of a huge family picnic.

As people arrived from the Goddess Mound, they spread out their blankets and chairs on the village green. Children began to eat, laugh and play games. The adults seemed to have become children for the day and they tried the games too, with a lot of laughing and cheering each other on.

Honey sat watching the feast and for the first time in the last couple of years, she actually felt part of the celebration, even part of the large family and she loved it.

"Are you having fun?" Ivy asked as she sat down next to Honey, passing her one of the two cups of orange juice she carried.

"Thanks...oh yes. Very much so, but I'm more happy that we are friends again." She smiled shyly at Ivy.

Ivy smiled back at her, "I am too." Ivy raised her cup towards Honey, "Happy Summer Solstice."

"Happy Summer Solstice." Honey replied and sipped her drink, "I wish I could come here more often, I love it here...it's so different from home."

"Well, why don't you?"

"I'd love to...but I'm not sure if I would be allowed." Honey said.

"Perhaps you could ask both our parents if you can visit more often, maybe at Yule? We have a lot of fun at Yule, you would like it here then too." Ivy said. She realised what she had just suggested, that Honey was to visit more often. If someone had told her that she would say that, last year or even last week, Ivy would not have believed them.

"Would you come with me to ask your parents?"

"Of course, let's do it now." Ivy grinned and stood up, determined to help make her cousin happy and get her to come more often.

The girls searched through the crowd for Ivy's parents, they found them by the drinks stand talking to Ash's parents, Lily and Thorn. After getting her parents to excuse themselves, Ivy lead them over to stand under the great oak on the far edge of the green, which was the quietest area and the girls nervously explained their idea.

"I think that's an excellent idea." Ivy's Father, Heath, said as he pushed his glasses back up his nose.

"So do I." Ivy's mum said, "I shall ring your parents when we get back today and see what they say. Now you girls go off and have some fun, okay?"

"Thanks, mum." Ivy said as they both headed off back to the party and Ivy's friends.

That evening, just before diner, while Honey was in the shower, Ivy sat in her small bedroom wondering at the quick change of events over the last few days, not only had they become friends again but now there was a possibility that they would see more of each other, that's if Honey got permission to visit at Yule. The thought of seeing Honey more was now a happy thought and Ivy looked at the camp bed wishing there was room for a spare bed in her bedroom but there just wasn't.

"Penny for your thoughts?" Ivy's mum asked as she stood in the doorway.

"Just thinking how nice it would be to spend more time with Honey." Ivy said.

"I'm glad to hear you say that as I have something I want to talk to you about before Honey comes back from the shower."

"What is it?"

"We have been talking to Honey's parents for sometime now about an idea we've had...we've suggested to them that Honey come and stay with us and go to school here in Brew, visiting her parents whenever they are in the country."

Ivy sat still, speechless.

"What do you think?" Mum asked.

Honey came out of the shower and headed downstairs for dinner, to find everyone already sat at the table waiting for her. The table was set with bowls of salad, cold chicken, fresh herb rolls and coleslaw, which was Honey's favourite meal.

"I'm sorry, am I late for dinner? I didn't hear anyone call me." She said as she sat opposite Ivy.

"No, no...you're here just in time." Cherry said, "Before we start, we need to talk to you about something, Honey."

Honey looked around nervously, had she done something wrong? She looked at Ivy who just looked down at her empty plate.

"It's okay, Honey, you're not in trouble." Cherry put her hand on Honey's as it sat limp and lifeless on the table. "We have been talking to your parents and amongst ourselves about an idea we've had, we have suggested to them that you come and stay with us permanently."

"Oh!" Honey said. She looked at her aunt, then her uncle and then at Ivy who was still looking down at her plate.

"You would go to school here in Brew with Ivy and her friends and visit your parents at home whenever you want to."

For a moment Honey was so surprised that her mind went blank.

"What do you think to the idea, Honey?" Cherry said.

"I...I...would love to...but will they let me? What about Ivy...it's her room after all. Do you want me to stay, Ivy?" Honey looked back at Ivy who was now looking directly at her.

"Of course." Ivy said with a huge smile on her face.

"We have thought of that, Heath will move his desk into the dinning room bay window and you can have his office as a bedroom."

"I...so...I would live with you? Like part of the family?" Ivy said.

"You're already part of the family, Honey." Ivy said.

"Exactly. Well said, Ivy." Heath said.

"Will my parents let me stay? What about my tutor, I mean they like me to be privately tutored." Honey said.

"Your parents have already agreed to it but only if you want to do it. They wanted you to know that they think the Elementary School here is excellent and they are very happy for you to have more family around you and of course, you can go back to visit them whenever you like. So you have a choice, you can carry on visiting us whenever you like or you can move in and visit you parents." Cherry smiled gently at Honey and patted her hand, she knew it must be a hard decision for Honey, "Do you need time to think about it, before you decide? We can, of course, try it for a few months if you're unsure." Cherry squeezed Honey's hand in encouragement.

"I...no, I want to stay." Honey said.

"Won't you miss your mum and dad and being in that big house?" Ivy said.

"No! I hate that big cold house...I will miss my mother and father, of course, but when I visit I will probably see them the same amount I do now and I get to be with everyone here...and...go to school." Honey said. Her face could hardly contain the huge smile it now held.

"Then it's agreed." Cherry stood and quickly moved over to Honey to hug her, "Welcome to your new home and to Brew, Honey."

Everyone cheered and many happy hugs followed before they all sat down to a celebration dinner, full of laughter and plans.

Ivy sat eating and looking around at her family, happy that she now understood that hospitality is more than just sharing her bedroom when she is told to. She could see how happy Honey had become by such an act of kindness. Ivy realised that hospitality is about giving freely to those that have a need, sharing what you have with those that have not and about doing these things happily, without expecting anything back in return.

She smiled to herself, proud of what her family had done, and began to ask Honey how she was going to arrange her things in the new bedroom.

Rowan the Hungry Witch

An Introduction to Rowan

Each of the children of Brew has been named after items in Nature and Rowan is no exception.

Named after the Rowan tree, which is also known as the Mountain Ash and the Witch Tree because of the pentagram that can be found at the base of its berries. The Rowan has always been regarded as an aid for protection against evil charms and enchantment. It's believed that if it's planted at the gate of your garden it will ward away evil spirits and if used as a walking stick it will protect the traveller from evil and guide him home safely. In addition, it's associated with astral travel, vision and healing. The berries and leaves can be dried and burned as incense to invoke spirits, familiars, spirit guides, and the elements.

Our Rowan is twelve years old, with short naturally curly brown hair and big brown eyes. She is a very good swimmer and is on the school swim team with her best friend Willow. Unfortunately, swimming makes her even more hungry and Rowan is always hungry. She has a slim build and is five foot tall.

This tale begins one week before Lughnasadh, otherwise known as First Harvest.

Rowan the Hungry Witch

Rowan breathed in deeply as she walked home from swimming practice. The air was warm and fragrant as she walked past her neighbour's gardens. There was something very special about a summer evening, the smells and sounds of life all around her. Rowan was happy.

In fact, Rowan's world was perfect in these moments.

Her best friend, Willow, had made it into the school's swim team and they got to practice together several days a week. Rowan thought it was nice to share a hobby with a friend.

The girls had just parted their ways at the street corner, Willow headed off towards her home and Rowan continued down the quiet country lane. The sound of the evening birds calling to each other kept her company during the short walk, that and the sound of her stomach loudly rumbling, the 'Beast Within' was obviously ready for dinner. A sudden waft of BBQ breezed by and Rowan turned to smelt it.

"Hmmm...I hope you're my dinner." She said out loud as if talking to the smell.

Rowan's family lived in the old converted barn at the end of the lane. She had lived there as long as she could remember, her parents, Rain and Poppy, had moved there just after she was born, and renovated the old barn into the beautiful home it now was. Her brother Calder and sister Opal, who were non-identical twins, were born in the house seven years ago tomorrow. Rowan loved her brother and sister very much, she loved everything about them from their flaming red hair to their fiery tempers, she had been overjoyed when they were born and enjoyed every minute she had with them since that day. Rowan believed that you know you love someone when you have a nickname for him or her and they love it two. Rowan called the twins the 'Monsters'. It suited them.

At last, she walked down the gravel drive that led to her house. Her stomach groaned with joy as she continued to smell the BBQ. She could hear the squeals of laughter from behind the house and a huge smile blossomed on her face. She ran the last few feet to the corner of the house and the side gate. The view that greeted her was a familiar one; Rowan's mum, Poppy, was on the ground soaked to the skin, her long auburn hair stuck to her face and neck, she was laughing and trying to squirt the water hose on the twins, the twins were sat on her while they had their water pistols pointed at Rain, their dad.

Rain, a tall, slim, dark haired man, grinned from ear to ear. "Wait, don't shoot! I need to turn the food!" He said breathlessly from laughing so hard. He was also soaked through, his t-shirt stuck to him like a second skin and his khaki shorts were dripping. His curly brown hair was stuck to his forehead and made rivulets of water run down his happy face.

"Hey, Monsters." Rowan called as she closed the gate behind her.

The twins looked round and finally spotted Rowan, grinning all the while.

"You get dad and I'll turn the food." Rowan threw her bags down against the side of the house and headed towards the large grill, which sat on the edge of the patio area.

The twins squealed with joy and ran for their dad shouting all the way.

"Traitor." Dad shouted to Rowan as he went down under the unstoppable force of the wet twins.

"Always." Rowan shouted back as she grabbed the pinchers from the rack and quickly turned the chicken and corn. "I think these are about done." She shouted over the excited noise.

Poppy stood up holding her ribs from laughter as she watched her husband struggle with Calder and Opal. She grabbed the hosepipe and gave them all a good soaking. The twins screeched as the cold water hit them.

Rain shouted "Hey, you're supposed to be on my side."

"Just cooling you all off before dinner." She laughed and turned off the hose. "Right then, towels are on the patio chairs, everyone go and grab one while I get the drinks and salad." Poppy walked into the house rubbing herself down with the towel and folded her hair up into it like a turban.

Supper was eaten outside on the patio while everyone finished drying off in the warm evening air. Rowan ate hers with absolute pleasure. She loved food and her stomach, or the 'Beast Within', was always growling for more. Dinner conversation was mostly about the plans for the twin's party the next day. The 'Monsters' were getting very excited.

"Rowan, I have to nip into the city first thing tomorrow, to pick up a few last minute things for the party. Do you want to come with me?" Mum said.

"Sure, we don't go into the city often. Might see something interesting." She said as she wiped the last of the butter, from the sweetcorn, off her chin.

"Can we come?" The twins said in unison.

"You promised to help your dad decorate the garden in time for your party. He has balloons."

"Balloons? Can we..." Opal said.

"...Blow them up?" Calder finished the sentence.

"I'm sure you can help in lots of ways." Dad said with a big smile.

The twins cheered and began to eat their homemade ice cream that their mum had just passed them before it melted.

After breakfast the following morning, Rowan and her mum, Poppy, set off on the hour's drive to the city in the family's small red car. Rowan hadn't been in the city for many months, living in the village of Brew meant that they needed very little from the city. They had their own shops, which sold only the local produce and their own school. The visits to town were also rare as Poppy looked after the house and the children so she didn't go out to work and Rain, Rowan's father, worked from home for the government via the internet. Not seeing it often made Rowan curious about the city, she was interested in it because it was different and yet she didn't like it, as it was dirty, with rubbish on the streets and hardly any trees.

"Why is the city so dark and dirty? Why don't they use the bins?" Rowan asked as she sadly looked out of the window at the littered streets.

"Many city dwellers don't think like us, Rowan. They don't believe that the Earth is a living breathing entity and that we are guests here. They think they can pollute her, waste her resources and even worse, think they can get away with it."

"Why don't we stop them?" Rowan said.

"Many have tried, over the years, but they won't listen. They don't believe us and they turn against our ways. It's one of the reasons why Sage Featherstone founded Brew, to give like minded people a place to live...in tune with the Mother and her seasons."

"I feel sorry for the people of the city, they are missing so much."

"So do I, Roo, so do I." Poppy smiled sadly at her daughter. She was proud that Rowan understood what they were missing.

Rowan's stomach growled loudly.

"You can't be hungry already! We just ate a large breakfast." Poppy said.

"I know but the 'Beast' seems to want more." Rowan said looking confused.

"There is an apple in my bag just behind my seat, if you can reach it."

Rowan carefully reached back, found the apple and began to munch on it.

"Is that better?" Poppy said.

Rowan nodded, chewing happily.

The apple was soon demolished and she placed the core in the car bin, which was a paper bag by her foot.

Rowan was obviously thinking hard about something, so much so that her mum said, "What are you thinking about, it looks pretty serious whatever it is."

"I was wondering why I'm always so hungry, Willow is never as hungry as I am. Is there something wrong with me?" Rowan looked worriedly at her mum.

"There is absolutely nothing wrong with you, you're a very healthy young lady." Poppy looked at her daughter, "You have to remember that at your age your body is going through some changes and one of them is your metabolism, it is speeding up, using your energy faster and so makes you feel more hungry. The best way to deal with it is not miss any meals because that will make it worse, obviously, and to eat a healthy snack in-between meals so that you don't overeat at each mealtime. The older you get the more your metabolism will slow down. All teenagers go through it, you are just getting it a little earlier than others...than Willow. I'm sure some of your other friends will get it soon too. It's perfectly normal Roo, don't worry about it." She smiled encouragingly.

"Hmmm...the apple did help. I wonder if any of my other friends are getting hungry too." Rowan said.

"You should ask them next Saturday."

"Saturday?"

"It's Lughnasadh, the First Harvest celebration next week." Poppy said.

"Oh yeah, I almost forgot. I like the First Harvest, the games are so much fun."

Rowan gazed out of her side window as Poppy drove through the main streets of the city until she reached a very poor area and pulled up outside a tatty run down house in the middle of a row of identical council houses.

"Who lives here?" Rowan asked, realising for the first time that she had no idea of who they had come to the city to see.

"Someone I went to college with, many years ago. His family have fallen on hard times and I thought I would help them out a bit by getting something for the party from them." Poppy said as she climbed out of the car.

Rowan got out the car and looked around, most of the street was dirty and depressing; some of the front yards were filled with broken down cars others were just filled with rubbish. Yet, strangely, there were others that were clean and tidy, full of summer flowers. It was an odd mix.

Rowan looked up at the house they had parked in front of and wondered what could this person have for the twin's birthday party? Rowan followed her mum up the garden path to the front door. On each side of the door there was a small strip of soil with plants in, the plants looked like vegetables, she thought they looked like lettuce, beetroot and carrots.

Rowan's attention was pulled back to the green painted front door as her mother knocked. A dog started barking loudly from within and she heard children shouting that someone was at the door.

A skinny man with wild hair and a bushy beard opened the door and peered out suspiciously. His face suddenly lit up with a huge smile and his eyes glowed with pleasure. "Poppy!" He said, his voice full of joy as he stepped out and hugged Rowan's mum enthusiastically.

Rowan was stunned, she had never met her mum's friend and for some reason didn't expect the friend to look like the man stood before her.

"Finch? Is that you under all that beard?" She laughed as she hugged him back.

"Sure is, Poppy. You look gorgeous as ever, country life suits you." He said. "And who is this?"

"Sorry...Finch, this is my daughter Rowan. Rowan, this is Finch the nearest thing I have to a brother." Poppy grinned happily.

"Nice to meet you Mr. Finch." Rowan said not sure how to take this wild man that her mum considered a 'brother'.

"It's just Finch, no 'Mr.' in front of it. It's very nice to meet you too Rowan, you look just like your mum did at your age." He said.

Rowan glanced at her mum.

"Finch and I grew up together and went to the same schools and college. We lost touch for a few years when he got a big job abroad but he has just come back." She explained.

"Come in, come in...we have lots to talk about and you have to meet Aster and the kids."

Rowan followed her mum and Finch into the small house. The inside was tidy and clean even if the furniture was old and well used. She was introduced to Aster, Finch's wife, a small rounded lady with long brown curly hair and very pale blue eyes. The children came rushing is to meet the visitor's, there were four; a baby girl who was only a few months old called Peri, a four year old boy called Seal, an eight year old girl whose name was Saffron and the eldest, at thirteen, was another boy, his name was Tim. They all seemed happy and excited and were soon shuffled out to the garden to play and work off their excited energy. The dog that Rowan had heard earlier, barked again when the door to the garden was opened. It must have been shut in the garden when we arrived, Rowan thought.

Rowan and her mum were shown to the living room and Poppy was soon lost in conversation with Finch and Aster. Rowan sat quietly on the sofa looking around the small room. Rowan spotted and began staring at the beautiful carved wooden statue of the Mother Goddess on the mantelpiece, over the empty fireplace. It was the most amazing thing she had ever seen, there were so many small details that she kept seeing new things every time her eyes looked over it. It was almost as if the statue was looking at her and her robes seemed to sway in the breeze. Rowan blinked at it, amazed.

Out of the corner of her eye Rowan saw Aster stand and leave the room while Poppy and Finch continued talking. Rowan walked over to the fireplace to look at the statue up close and Aster soon returned with cold drinks for everyone. "I've asked Tim to fetch..." She glanced at Poppy and Rowan. "Does she know?"

"Not yet." Poppy smiled.

"Ah...well, Tim will be back in a minute then." Aster sat back down next to her husband with a knowing look on her face.

"Do you like my statue?" Finch said as he got up and walked over to the fireplace.

"I think it is awesome. Where did you get it?" Rowan said.

"I made it." He smiled and his face lit up again, this time with pride.

Rowan couldn't help but like this wild man, "Wow." It was all she could think of saying.

"You made it?" Poppy said as she stood and joined them, taking a closer look. "This is amazing, I had no idea you carved wood. This is seriously good. Do you sell them?"

"Yes, but no one is buying them here. Not much call for the Mother Goddess in the city." He said.

"Hmmm..." Poppy said.

Finch laughed. "I remember that sound. What are you thinking?" He said.

"Well...I..."

Before Rowan's mum could finish her sentence Tim burst into the room with his arms full of fluff, at least that's what it seemed like to Rowan, at first. Tim placed the bundle of fluff on the floor and it slowly unfurled to reveal a sleepy puppy. It was mainly black with white and brown patches on its face, brown just above its paws and a white neck and stomach. It had huge brown eyes and was incredibly adorable. As soon as its eyes were open it jumped up and ran round the room sniffing everyone.

Rowan squealed with delight and stroked its soft fur.

"This is the twin's birthday present, he's a Burmese Mountain dog. Do you like him?"

"Oh wow, he's awesome. What's his name?" Rowan said.

"He doesn't have one yet." Tim replied with a smile as he sat on the floor next to Rowan and played with the puppy.

Rowan and Tim sat stroking the puppy's tummy whilst the adults were in deep conversation again. Sitting so close to Tim made Rowan nervous in a strange way, she wasn't sure why. She heard a tummy rumble and knew it wasn't hers for a change. Tim looked a little embarrassed and looked at his mum, "Do we have any apples left? I'm hungry."

"No you had the last one yesterday." Aster said.

Poppy glanced at Rowan with a knowing smile.

"Anything else I can eat?" Tim said.

"Not until I go shopping again next week. I don't think there are any more carrots ready in the front yet, we've picked most of them. Try drinking some water it may help." His mum said.

"I'll be okay." He mumbled, looking even more embarrassed.

Rowan felt awkward and felt sorry for him because she knew how hungry she felt sometimes.

"I get hungry all the time too." She said quietly with a shy smile.

"You do?" He looked at her surprised.

"Yes. My mum says it because my metabo...something is working faster the older I get."

"Metabolism?" He said.

"Yes, that's it. She says it's normal."

"Still knowing that doesn't make the hunger go away, does it?" He smiled sadly at her, "I try not to ask too often for stuff, and since dad got laid off there has been less food. I was thinking of getting a paper round to help out." He whispered.

"That's a good idea...sorry about your dad."

"Thanks." Tim said as he rubbed the puppy's tummy.

"Well, I'm afraid we have to go. I have to get ready for the twins party. Did you manage to get your car fixed? I would love to see you all there." Poppy said.

"Yes, we did. It was something simple and cheap for once." Finch grinned, "We shall see you about four and I have your phone number now, if we get lost."

Aster picked up the puppy and put him in an animal carrier ready for the journey home. Poppy gave Aster some money, although it looked to Rowan like she didn't want to take it, then the whole family saw us out to the car waving goodbye to us and the puppy.

"See you later." Tim said to Rowan with a big smile that made his eyes light up like his dad's.

Rowan blushed and said, 'bye' in a small nervous voice and closed the car door.

During the drive home Rowan was quiet, she couldn't stop thinking about Tim not just because he was nice and made her oddly nervous but because he was hungry all the time like her.

"What are you thinking about now, Roo?" Poppy asked. "You seem to be lost in thoughts today."

"About Tim."

"Nice boy isn't he?" Poppy said.

"Mum!" Rowan blushed. "Yes, no...I mean...I was thinking about how he's hungry all the time like I am."

"See, I told you others get it too and it's normal."

"I believed you. I felt sorry for him because they had nothing to eat to make it go away." Rowan said.

"Money is very tight for them right now, especially with neither of his parents working."

"It makes me sad to think about it. I know there are poor hungry people around the world, we were taught that at school, but knowing there is some here...near us...it makes me feel bad."

"It is very sad. When Finch got laid off, they lost the house which came with his job and they had to move back home and, with no income, had to go into council housing." Poppy said. "They are not the only ones, there are many poor people in most cities, and there are even some in the villages surrounding Brew."

"Can't we do something to help them?" Rowan looked hopefully at her mum.

"Hmmm...maybe we can. I will talk to your dad about it when we get home. Do you think the twins will love the puppy?"

Rowan glanced at the back seat where the carrier was strapped in. "Absolutely." She couldn't wait until they got home to see the 'Monsters' reaction.

The drive home seemed shorter and than the drive out, funny how it's always like that. Before Rowan knew it, they were pulling up their drive and down the side of the house to the garage. Poppy and Rowan climbed out of the car just as dad and the twins burst from the house to greet them. Poppy hauled the carrier out of the car and placed it gently on the ground.

"Rain, can you close the gate, please?" Poppy Said.

Rowan's dad quickly closed the gate at the side of the house and returned.

"This is a very special present for your birthday from the three of us." Poppy said to the twins. "Be very gentle."

The twins got closer to the carrier but all they could see was fur.

"Hello?" They said in unison.

Rowan laughed and knelt down by the carrier, "It can't talk, silly." She opened the carrier and waited just a moment as everyone looked at it. With a rush and a blur of fur the puppy shot out and began licking Opal who squealed in delight, it then turned its attention to Calder and jumped on him licking him too. The twins erupted in unstoppable giggles as they played with and stroked the puppy, in return they were covered in friendly licks.

"You have to find a name for him because he doesn't have one yet." Poppy said as she happily watched them playing.

The twins stopped for a moment and looked at each other, and without conferring, they both said "Jack".

Their parents laughed and looked a bit startled, "Why Jack?" Dad said.

"Jack in..." Calder said.

"...a box." Opal said.

They both pointed to the carrier.

Rowan laughed, "Well that makes sense." She walked over and knelt down to play with them.

"That was easier than I thought." Dad said.

"No kidding." Mum said. "The garden looks lovely by the way." She reached over and kissed his cheek affectionately.

"Thanks, the twins helped a lot."

Rowan looked round the trees and buses, which were full of balloons, streamers and paper lanterns. She thought it looked like a perfect place to hold a birthday party.

Throughout the afternoon, families arrived with food to share and presents for the twins. Soon the garden was full of talking, laughter and children playing. Finch, Aster and family arrived and while the children played, the adults sat on the patio and talked and talked. Several of the Elders had arrived at the party and were also talking to Finch and Aster. Eventually, the puppy, Jack, became very tired and fell asleep on the grass. Rowan and Tim had the job of trying to keep the younger children away from him for a little while so he could rest.

Again Tim made Rowan feel nervous but in a nice way and eventually her nervousness began to go away as they sat and talked.

"Nice house." Tim said.

"Thanks."

"It's quiet out here in the country, do you like it?"

"Yes, I love it. Can't imagine living anywhere else. We have our own school too, I'm on the swim team." Rowan said proudly.

"Cool. I like swimming but since we moved there is nowhere to swim nearby."

"Come here more often and we can swim in the river." She offered.

"I'd like that, thanks." He said and smiled.

Eventually, the party came to an end and all the guests left, including Finch and his family. That evening the twins were so tired that they went to bed earlier than usual. After Rowan helped clear up, she sat with her mum outside. Rowan picked up and snuggled Jack on her lap, smiling at how the twins wanted him to sleep in their room.

"I think they loved their pressie, mum."

"I think they did too." She smiled happily and poured herself a glass of red wine.

"Where's dad?" Rowan said.

"He just went to talk to some of the Elders, he'll be back soon. Why?"

"Just wondered."

"I invited Finch and his family to the First Harvest celebration and the Lughnasadh games next weekend."

"Cool. Are they coming?"

"Yes."

Rowan heard the gate close and her father came around the corner of the house with a big smile on his face.

"It's done." He said and flopped happily into the nearest chair.

"What's done, dad?"

"You know the old cottage that's sitting empty, in the back field of Elders' Wolf and Violets farm?" He said.

"Yes, the white one?"

"That's it. Well, Wolf and Violet have agreed to let Finch and his family live there if he works for them on the farm." He said with a satisfied grin.

"They're moving here?" Rowan said surprised and looked at each of her parents.

"They are now. I'd best go and ring Finch and let him know Wolf and Violet said yes. They'll be so pleased." Poppy said as she excitedly jumped out of her chair and headed into the house.

"That's great." Rowan said as she stroked Jack behind the ear. A little flutter of excitement swirled in her stomach knowing that Tim would be around a lot more. "When will they be moving here?"

"I'm not sure. The cottage needs a lot of cleaning up. It's not been lived in for many years, the chimney needs mending and there's a small leak in the roof but the building is sound."

A few moments later Poppy came back out from the house, "They're so happy and excited." She sank back into her chair. "They will go and take a look at the cottage to see what needs doing next weekend, when they're here for Lughnasadh."

"Oh, I've just remembered something I need to tell Willow, I'm just going to ring her." Rowan placed Jack in Poppy's arms and ran inside to use the phone.

Rowan spent the next week out and about with her friends. Her parents barely saw her, which was not unusual for this time of year when school was out. Poppy, Rain and the twins only got to catch up with Rowan at table during their evening meal. Most days, Rowan was with Willow and they had been doing their favourite thing, swimming in the river that ran alongside the village of Brew. It was a great way to cool off during the summer heat and to practise for the school team.

It seemed to Rowan that the weekend of Lughnasadh came around rather quickly and before she knew it, she was standing with her family on the edge of the village Green watching some of the games. Rowan loved Lughnasadh; it was the celebration of the God Lugh, Lord of the Harvest and of Craftsmen, of the Mother Goddess who made the ground fertile, and of the first harvest of the year. She loved how everything they were celebrating was linked together.

Every year in Brew, Lughnasadh is celebrated with many summer games including archery, arm wrestling, horseshoe throwing, tug-of-war and many more. All of these games are held on the Village Green, the road around the central Green area is closed to traffic and the villagers are able to watch the games by bringing folding chairs and sitting on the road. Dotted throughout the Village Green were people selling drinks, ice cream and freshly made sandwiches for the spectators and competitors. Everyone joined in by either cheering the spectators on or by entering the competitions.

Lughnasadh was a full day of celebration. In the morning before, the day got too warm, the games were played and finished by lunch when everyone relaxed and chatted, then it was onto the Goddess Mound, so named because it looked a pregnant stomach rising into the sky. The Goddess Mound had a long winding path that led to the top and upon the top were thirteen ancient stones pointing up to the sun, like massive blades of grass. Within this circle of stones the thirteen elders of Brew would perform the Lughnasadh ritual. After the ritual the Elders would announce the large feast back on the Village Green where they would also give out the names of the winners of the games. It was traditional for every family to bring food to share at the feast.

Rowan walked over and sat down with the 'Monsters' on the grass, at the edge of the Green watching the games. Jack had been left at home today because he was still a bit too young and not trained well enough for such a big crowd. Rowan's eye roamed the people around her and she blushed as she spotted Tim with his family, making their way towards Rowan's parents. She was so pleased they had come for the day but for some weird reason she could not stop looking at Tim.

"Roo...Roo!" The twins chimed.

"Huh?" Rowan turned back to the twins.

"Roo, he's here. He's here." They said.

"I know I just saw him, I think they are putting up chairs near mum and dad." Rowan strained her neck to try to see but the crowd was stood up applauding something.

"You're looking the wrong way." Calder said.

"He's over there." Opal said excitedly.

"Who is?" Rowan turned to see where they were pointing and suddenly realised why everyone was clapping. John Barleycorn, or rather a man dressed as him, had walked out onto the Green. The man wore barley straw everywhere, like a scarecrow, it was tucked into his shirt and trousers and stuck out at his wrists and bare feet. You could barely see his face for the corn stalks, just his eyes twinkled out. John Barleycorn danced around the competitors, silently cheering them on, then he danced out into the crowd where people touched him for luck. Rowan looked forward to seeing him in the ritual later and wondered if Tim knew about John Barleycorn.

By lunchtime, the games had finished and the people of Brew settled down to a picnic lunch together. Rowan and the twins returned to their family, she was pleased to find Tim, his brother, sisters and Finch and Aster were all there. The children waved and smiled as they approached, but Rowan only noticed Tim's smile. It made her feel wall warm and fuzzy, so much so that she nearly tripped over the kerb. She righted herself, blushed furiously and sat down quickly, trying not to look round to see if anyone saw her do it.

A little while after the simple lunch, Rowan heard the horn blow from the Goddess Mound calling all the villagers to ritual. Everyone quickly packed up their belongings and left them in neat piles around the Green, for collection later. Rowan's and Tim's family joined the stream of people now walking down the lane towards the mound. Rowan walked with the twins in front of the others. Along the way the villagers were happily chatting amongst themselves until the reached the start of the path that led up the mound. As soon as they stepped onto the sacred mound a hush fell over them and they climbed round and up and up and round in a companionable silence.

Rowan and the two families finally reached the top and, like everyone else, were drummed onto the mound by the local musical group, Moon Scape. They walked past the drummers and stood with the other villagers outside of the ring of stones. The Elders were stood inside the stone circle and each one was dressed in a golden robe, the colour of harvested corn. Within the circle sat the altar, which was also made of stone. Upon the altar was a large man made of bread and a large corn dolly made from the first ears of this year's harvested barleycorn. Beside the altar was the large firepit, already lit by Elder Birch, a large man with a big bushy beard who is Brew's firekeeper.

The drumming stopped and a silence full of anticipation filled the circle. Two of the Elders stepped away from their respective stones and walked across the circle to stand in front of the altar.

Rowan recognised the two Elders, they were Elder Daisy, the Mistress of Women's Mysteries, a small, curvy woman with one of those faces that never stops smiling. She had shoulder length thick hair, which was wavy and totally silver. The other was Elder Furze, Master of the Men's Mysteries, a thin, very straight standing man with short dark hair and piercing blue eyes, he had what seemed to be a severe face until he smiled and his face was transformed into kindness itself. These Elders were two of Rowan's favourites and they traditionally performed the Lughnasadh ritual every year.

"Welcome everyone to our Lughnasadh celebration, the celebration of the First Harvest." Elder Furze said in a strong voice as he held his hands up in the air with enthusiasm.

The crowd erupted in a joyful cheer.

Elder Daisy raised her arms in the air and slowly lowered them, once again a hush filled the stone circle. "Lughnasadh is also a time of personal reflection and the harvest of our actions and deeds that we have 'planted' this year. The harvest of what we have sown though trial, tribulation, enjoyment, joy, love and loss." She said and looked at Elder Furze.

"At Lughnasadh we celebrate the harvest with the story John Barleycorn and his tale of the life mysteries that play out each year during the seasons. John Barleycorn also reminds us that levity, joy and festivity are as much a part of our lives as Death and Rebirth." Elder Furze paused, "I give you the Brew Mummers."

As the last word fell from Elder Furze lips, John Barleycorn leapt into the inner circle of the stones to a rousing applause. He made several playful bows and Moon Scape began to play his song as three men, dressed as farmers with scythes also appeared in the circle. All four men began to act out the words of the song, which were being sung by all the Elders, the villagers soon joined in with the singing.

'There came three men from out the West
Their victory to try,
And they have taken a solemn oath
John Barleycorn should die.
Sing ri fol lol, the diddle al the dee,
Right fal leero dee.

They took a plough and ploughed him in,
Laid clods upon his head:
And they have taken a solemn oath
John Barleycorn is dead.
So then he lay for a full fortnight

Till the dew from the sky did fall:
John Barleycorn sprung up again
And that surprised them all.

But when he faced the summer sun
He looked both pale and wan,
For all he had a spiky beard
To show he was a man.

But soon came men with sickles sharp
And chopped him to the knee.
They rolled and tied him by the waist
And served him barb'rously.

With forks they stuck him to the heart
And banged him over stones,
And sent the men with holly clubs
To batter at his bones.

But Barleycorn has noble blood,
It lives when it is shed.
It turns a tinker to a lord
It fills the empty head.

It makes the widow's heart to sing,
And it turns the coward bold:
It fills the cupboard and the purse
With bread and meat and gold.

Sing ri fol lol, the diddle al the dee,
Right fal leero dee.' [1]

At the end of the song all four men stood holding horns of barley beer raising a toast to Lugh, God of the Harvest and to the Mother Goddess, without whom John Barleycorn could never grow. The crowd cheered and said 'Hail'.

The Elders continued with the ritual but Rowan couldn't tear her eyes away from Tim who stood with wide eyes and a huge smile on his face. He had obviously never seen it before and really enjoyed the Brew Mummers performing John Barleycorn. Rowan remembered the first time she had seen it as a child, and wondered if the look on her face had been the same.

"Before we make the sacrifice of the corn, we want to welcome to our community, a new family." Elder Daisy said as she and Elder Furze stepped forward until they stood just in front of Finch and his family.

"A huge welcome to Finch and Aster, and to their children Timber, Saffron, Seal and little Peri." Elder Daisy said.

"Welcome to each of you." Elder Furze said.

Once again the crowd cheered and shouted 'welcome' as the Elders hugged everyone.

Finch and Aster had huge smiles on their faces, Tim looked a bit embarrassed and the rest of the children, except Peri who was in her mother's arms feeding, looked around them wondering what was happening.

"Timber? I didn't know that was your name." Rowan whispered in Tim's ear.

"Yeah, I prefer Tim though, thanks." He smiled sheepishly at her.

"Then Tim it is." She smiled back at him, happy to make him less embarrassed.

The Elders walked back to the altar and picked up the huge bread loaf shaped like a man, it was about the same size as Rowan.

"Our very deepest thanks go out to our baker, Elder Brook and his wife Elder Camellia, for our Bread Man. Please everyone, come forward and break off a piece of bread, taking a piece for yourself and a piece for the Ancestors." Furze said.

The villagers began to move into the circle walking around the back of the altar and then curving around to the front, each breaking off a piece of the Bread Man and then splitting it in half. They placed one piece in their mouths and the other into the fire, returning the harvest back to the soil and to the ancestors. They then spiralled round the inside of the circle until they filtered back outside of the stones taking up their original positions.

Rowan found this fascinating to watch, it was like a human serpent winding its way around the stones, the fire and the Elders.

At last, it was Rowan's turn; she followed her family and took her place in the spiral. Finch and his family followed closely behind them, they seemed to be greatly enjoying themselves by the look on their faces.

Eventually, the entire village had taken into themselves a piece of the Bread Man and made an offering. Everyone returned to the outside of the circle of stones.

Elder Furze and Elder Daisy said their final words of blessing and thanked the Gods, closing the ritual. Elder Daisy then stepped slightly forward. "The celebration feast will begin in one hour on the Green as is usual for Lughnasadh, but before we leave the sacred circle, I would like to make an announcement." She smiled at the crowd. "As you may know, with the enormous help of two families Finch, Aster and the children are able to live within our village as well as being members of our community. A huge debt of thanks goes out to Rain, Poppy and Elders Violet and Wolf for finding a home for our new friends."

A great cheer went up from the crowd and a round of applause rippled round the circle. Both couples smiled and nodded their thanks.

Elder Daisy held up her hands to quiet the villagers. "However, what you don't know is that there is a little more to this story, something that's makes it just a bit more special." She looked around the circle of expectant faces. "Can Rowan and Willow please join me?" She looked directly at Rowan.

Rowan swallowed hard, for some reason her throat had suddenly gone dry. She took a deep breath and stepped out in front of everyone and walked towards Elder Daisy. She saw Willow also walking in the same direction, she was blushing furiously, and her red cheeks stood out brightly against her fair hair and made her green eyes even brighter. They finally reached the side of Elder Daisy and nervously held hands.

"Thanks to an idea that originated with Rowan, these two have been very industrious during this past week." She smiled proudly at the girls.

Rowan caught a glimpse of her parent's faces', surprise and confusion warred on their features. She saw a glimpse of pride on Elder Violet's face but she didn't dare look at anyone else.

"Through the kindness of their hearts and true effort on their part, they have worked tirelessly in a huge effort know only by two others. They have been sweeping, scrubbing, washing, whitewashing and generally cleaning the cottage that Finch and Aster's family are to live in, so that they can move in as soon as they bring their belongings."

The crowd exploded with 'ooh's' and 'ahh's' and then sudden applause thundered around the stones. The three families of Tim, Rowan and Willow surged forward offering their thanks and praise for such a kind act. The girls were hugged, patted on the back by everyone and hugged again. Rowan caught Tim's eye, he didn't hug her but looked at her and mouthed 'Thank you' and smiled his best smile. Rowan knew she they had done a good thing and made his family happy.

Finally, many of the villagers came up and congratulated the girls and then they began to drift off back down the mound to get ready for the evening feast.

"I'm so proud of you, Roo." Poppy said as she hugged her daughter for the fourth time.

"Thank you." Rowan beamed at her mum.

"Why don't we all go down to the cottage and take a look at the girls work before the feast, we have plenty of time." Rowan's dad suggested, smiling proudly.

"Excellent idea." Finch said.

The four families; Rowans', Willow's, Tim's and Elders Violet and Wolf began to walk back down the Goddess Mound, past the Green where some people were setting up long tables for the feast and onwards, down the winding country lane to Elders' Violet and Wolf's farm. They walked around the main buildings and out into one of the fields following the dirt track. The two-story cottage and its whitewashed walls shone in the late afternoon sunlight and stood out gloriously from the woodland behind it. There was a walled off area of garden both at the front and back, either garden was big enough to grow some vegetables and for the children to play.

Inside the cottage, the downstairs consisted of the hall, a bathroom, lounge and kitchen/dinning room. Everything was clean and tidy, and the rooms seemed huge without furniture. Tim and his brother and sister ran upstairs to check out the bedrooms.

"I fixed the chimney over the range last week and there is a small leak in the roof that I'll work on tomorrow but apart from that, it's now liveable, thanks to the girls hard work." Said Elder Wolf, a small man with a ruddy complexion and curly grey hair.

"This is wonderful!" Aster said as she placed Peri on her hip and ran her fingers over the old range.

"I don't know what to say...the kindness of you all is...overwhelming." Finch said.

"Isn't that what friends are for? Helping each other out even when it's hard to ask for help." Poppy said and hugged her life-long friend.

"And we desperately need some help on the farm so consider you lodgings as part of your wages and the rest we shall pay you in farm produce, if you're agreeable." Wolf said and held out his hand to Finch.

"Definitely, thank you. Thank you all. This means so much to me and my family." He hugged his wife happily.

"You could sell your carvings too." Rowan said.

"What a good idea." Finch said and beamed at her.

Aster handed Peri to Finch and said, "Thank you Rowan and Willow, for doing all this hard work and in secret too. You are wonderful girls." Aster hugged the girls gratefully in one big hug.

"Yes, just how did you keep it from us?" Rowan's dad said.

Rowan grinned. "We packed working clothes in with our swimming stuff, worked all day and then changed and swam before coming home to wash the dirt off."

Tim arrived back in the kitchen just in time to hear Rowan's comment. "Smart thinking." He said.

"Thanks." Rowan said and began to blush again. She discreetly turned away while everyone was talking and walked outside pretending to look at the weeds growing in the front garden, until her face stopped feeling flushed.

"You still blushing?" Poppy said from behind her.

"Mum!" Rowan blushed again.

"Okay, okay. You did a good thing, Roo. I'm so very proud of you."

"Thanks."

Rowan sat on the old stone wall and her mum sat down beside her, looking at her daughters face.

"What are you plotting now?" Poppy said.

"I was thinking about food."

Her mum laughed. "Now that's not a surprise. Don't worry, it will soon be time to eat."

"No. I am hungry but I was not thinking about my food. I was thinking about others like me who are hungry, but who have families like Tim's who don't have any extra food." Rowan said.

"Ah...yes, it's very sad that some people, many in fact, struggle to buy food."

"Hmmm..."

"Hmmm?" Poppy raised an eyebrow and looked at her daughter.

"You said there were several families in the villages around Brew that struggle, is that true?"

"Yes, sadly. Why?"

"I'm thinking about starting a Food Bank for them, what do you think?" She said and looked her mum in the eyes.

"Oh, that's a wonderful idea. I'm sure many people in Brew will join in. What an excellent way to help them." Poppy said as she hugged her daughter close, so proud of her that tears came to her eyes. "I love you."

"I love you too. Mum." Rowan hugged her back, "Now can we go to the feast? I'm hungry." Rowan said with a huge smile just as the 'Beast Within' rumbled.

---

[1] *John Barleycorn's song is an altered version of the song 'John Barleycorn: A Ballad' by Robert Burns.*

Hazel the Unwise Witch

An Introduction to Hazel

For many years, each child of Brew has been named after various items within Nature and Hazel is no exception. Named after the Hazel tree, which is considered one of the most important trees. It is very closely related to the salmon that eats its nuts of poetic wisdom and its associations are: intuition, poetry, divination, meditation, wisdom, knowledge and fertility.

Hazel is a fun loving girl who doesn't understand the consequences of rash decisions. She likes doing things without a safety net, such as riding her bike without her helmet and not looking as she crosses the road. Even though Hazel's parents and her friends tell her that she isn't invincible and that she would one day get hurt, she just thinks they worry too much for no good reason.

Hazel is about to celebrate being twelve years old on September 21st, the Autumn Equinox. She is a little small for her age and slim, has short curly black hair and beautiful skin, the colour of milk chocolate. Her eyes are a lovely hazelnut colour, which funnily suits her name.

Our tale begins a few days before the Autumn Equinox, otherwise known as Mabon. This is a time of Harvest Home when the nights are getting longer and cooler as we head towards those cosy winter nights.

Hazel the Unwise Witch

Hazel stretched and yawned as she lay in her bed thinking what she was going to do today. It was a few days before her twelfth birthday and she was beginning to get really excited. Her birthday was on the very day that Brew, the village in which her family lived, also celebrated the festival of the Autumn Equinox, otherwise known as Mabon. She knew that today the villagers would be busy preparing the decorations for the festival day and the village green would begin its transformation into a place of feasting and fun.

Hazel's family were no exception to the decorating fever. Right now, her parents were devising ways of decorating the house and garden for her birthday as well as the last harvest of the year. Meanwhile, her older brother, by only one year, Drake, was going to help his friends from school decorate the village green this morning.

"Hmmm....what shall I do today?" Hazel wondered. "I know." She sat up ready to get out of bed and caught a glimpse of herself in the mirror on her dresser. She cringed and looked away. Although she mostly liked her appearance, her morning hair was a frightening thing. She thought that with short wiry, curly hair, she always woke up looking like she had been dragged through a hedge backwards and the struggle had resulted in 'mad professor' hair, as she called it.

Hazel immediately jumped in the shower, it was the only thing that could tame her wild hair.

Once clean and hair suitably tamed, she rushed down to eat breakfast with her family, knowing she was running a little late, again. Rune, the family cat, laid stretched out on the bottom step of the stairs. Hazel adored cats and especially loved Rune with her blue-grey fur. As she whizzed past she plucked Rune from the step, lifted her up into her arms and stroked her thick fur as she walked through the hallway to the kitchen.

The kitchen was old and well used, the cupboards were all wooden and a deep honey colour. Hazel's mum and dad had painted the kitchen walls a warm yellow so that when the sun shone in through the large multi-pained window, as it did now, the room seemed to glow.

Hazel loved their kitchen, it made her feel happy every morning.

"Oh Great, Hazel the Unwise has graced us with her presence." Drake snickered as he bowed his head in mock respect. "I was about to eat your bacon." He said as he smirked at her over his empty plate, gleefully calling her by her nickname.

Hazel seemed to have spent her entire life being called 'the unwise' from her brother, it was usually followed by an adult saying to her; 'What are you doing?' or 'Why did you do that?' She hated the name and she thought people worried just a bit too much about what she was doing from one day to the next. She couldn't understand why they worried so. She 'knew' that the traffic would stop for her, just like she 'knew' she wouldn't fall off her bike when not wearing a helmet and she 'knew' that the lightening wouldn't strike the tree when she stood her under it.

Hazel glared at her brother, "Mum! That's not fair, he called me it again and he was going to eat my bacon." Hazel said as she let Rune slip out of her arms and sat down heavily at the kitchen table, opposite Drake.

"Drake, stop annoying your sister." Mum said as she poured orange juice in the glass in front of Hazel, "You know the rules in this house, Hazel. If you can't be bothered to come and eat when we do, you can go without." Hazel's mum, Pearl, was a woman with the coveted curves of the Goddess and a happy outlook on life, usually.

"I'm here now...almost on time."

"Only just." said Drake, still eyeing her bacon. "Dad has already left for work, two more minutes and that would have been mine." He grinned with a mean twinkle in his eye. Like any brother, Drake loved to annoy his sister, no matter how much trouble he got into for it.

Hazel ignored him and began tucking into her breakfast of bacon and scrambled eggs with toast. As she ate she decided that she would see if Rowan, her best friend, was busy today and if she wanted to bike out to Elder Bear's house to collect the mushrooms, which he was drying for their festival decorations.

Hazel loved the woods and in particular loved mushrooms, she knew that once the celebrations were over her mum would de-string the mushrooms and re-hydrate them for making her thick mushroom soup. Hazel loved her mum's mushroom soup more than she loved the woods and that was saying a lot.

Rowan met Hazel at the edge of the village green where the older boys were helping to put up the bunting - a string of small harvest colour flags. They fastened them to the big oak in the centre of the green and then spread them out towards the pub, the post office, the butcher's shop and the bakery. Each of the businesses were also decorating around their doors, windows and displays. Images of Harvest Home were appearing everywhere.

Rowan stood by her bike as Hazel rode towards her. She was dressed in old jeans, a pale blue t-shirt and, because the day was warm, instead of wearing her hoodie she had it tied around her waist. She didn't see Hazel approach as she was watching Elder Furze, the Master of Men's Mysteries, and the boys working on the decorations.

Hazel was struck again at how much Rowan looked like her. They both had curly hair, Rowan's was brown whereas Hazel's was black. They both had the same hazel coloured eyes and they were both small and slim. The only real difference being that Rowan's skin was pale with rosy cheeks, whilst Hazel's was a warm milk chocolate colour. They had been friends since they were very small, in fact, since their mum's met and became friends just after they were both born.

"Hiya!" Called Hazel as she applied her brakes and came to a stop next to her friend.

"Hi." Rowan said, "Your brother keeps looking over here with that smug look on his face. Did he get your breakfast again this morning?" She laughed and turned away from the boys, hopped on her bike and began to peddle away.

Hazel soon caught up, "No, beat him to it this morning. I don't think it was me he was looking at though, Roo." Hazel grinned as Rowan turned to give her a dirty look.

"Shut up." Rowan said and looked away blushing

They cycled along the main street and off onto Tillman's Lane, which headed towards the woods and Elder Bear's home.

"You should put that helmet on, someone might see you and tell ya mum." Rowan called over her shoulder.

"Nah, don't need it. I'm a careful cyclist." Hazel glanced at her helmet in her basket, which sat ignored on top of the cloth bag she had brought for the mushrooms. As soon as Hazel had got out of sight of her house, she had removed the helmet and thrown it into it's usual place in her basket, where it would stay until she put it back on when just around the corner from home again, as usual.

"I know you're a safe cyclist, but what about me?" Rowan said as they left the road and headed up the dirt track on the edge of the woods. Rowan wobbled all the way along the lumpy track.

"Just keep a good distance between us, then if you fall off I won't run you over. Well, not by accident anyway." Hazel said with a grin as the track got smaller and smaller, until there was only room to go single file and Hazel carefully followed her friend.

"Thanks for the encouragement." Rowan laughed.

Finally, the track turned a corner and opened up into a flat area of land that had been cleared of trees. The remains of the track turned into a path around the grassy area, which had wooden chairs scattered about and a small fire pit. Behind it sat the house belonging to Elder Bear, not a house exactly but more of a cabin. The small wooden structure nestled into the trees and bushes like it had grown there by itself.

Elder Bear, the co-leader of the Elders of Brew, was a big burly man with long, thick brown hair that when seen in a certain light had red strands in it. He stood outside his cabin placing bottles into wooden crates, looking up as the girls approached, he waved and then pushed his knuckles into the small of his back and rubbed it.

"Hello, girls. How are you both on this beautiful day?" His deep voice boomed in a friendly way from his bushy beard.

"Hello, Elder Bear." Hazel called as they neared.

"Hello!" Rowan said.

"I guess you have come for the dried mushrooms." He said.

Both girls laid down their bikes on the grass and walked over.

"Yes, we thought we would save you the trouble of bring them over today, Elder." Hazel said as she peered into the almost full crate.

"Well, 'tis kind of ya lasses." His big smile spread across his face.

"Are these your homemade wines for the Mabon celebration?" Hazel said.

"Yes, ya guessed right lass. This year we've got Blueberry, Peach and Raspberry." He said proudly as he held up a bottle against the sun, checking the colour of it.

"They sound tasty." Said Rowan.

"They will be lass, they will be and if you're very lucky both your parents might let you have a wee taste of 'em." His eyes twinkled as his face crumpled into another huge smile.

Hazel grinned back at him and was mesmerized, she loved the way his green eyes shone when he smiled and a smile could usually be found on Elder Bear's face.

"The 'shrooms are on the dryin' trays on the kitchen table, go on in and help yaselves those ones are all for the decorations. I want to finish packin' these." He said as he went back to packing the last of the bottles in the crate.

"Thanks." Hazel called back to him and headed towards the house.

The inside of the cabin was larger than it appeared from the outside, all the furniture was wooden as were the doors and the kitchen cupboards. The kitchen was at one end of the lounge and there were two doors leading from it. Hazel presumed they led to a bathroom and bedroom. The huge wooden kitchen table dominated the kitchen and laid out on it were several drying trays with many, many shrivelled up mushrooms.

The girls carefully collected all the mushrooms, placed them in the cloth bags they had brought and made their way back outside.

"Ya got them all?" Elder Bear asked.

"Yes, thanks." Hazel said.

"I'll look forward to my end of the barter with ya mam, her 'shroom soup is the best I've had." He grinned.

"I'll tell her that." Hazel said as she climbed back onto her bike.

"Do that. Aren't ya gonna wear your 'elmit like Rowan is? Ya might wanna save what cells ya 'ave up 'ere." He pointed to his head.

"Nah, I never fall off and I'm very careful too."

"Suit yaself, although ya mam may not agree."

"What she doesn't see, she doesn't know about." Hazel said over her shoulder as both girls began to cycle back down the bumpy track, calling goodbye.

"Don't bank on it, lass." Elder Bear said as he shook his head and watched them cycle back towards the village.

It wasn't long before the two girls reached the village green again, where this time the boys and Elder Furze were sat in the shade of the old oak drinking cold lemonade due to the unusually warm weather for the middle of September.

"Girls you look very warm, why not join us for a cooling drink?" Elder Furze called as the girls neared the green. His wild grey hair gently moved in the warm breeze as he began to prepare two more drinks from the picnic basket beside him.

The girls didn't have to be asked twice. They laid down their bikes on the edge of the green and came to sit under the shade of the big oak.

"Thank you, Elder Furze." Rowan said.

"Yes, thanks...hmmm...this is lovely lemonade, did you make it?" Hazel asked.

"By the Gods, no." He laughed as he twisted his long grey beard around his fingers, "My wife did, she is the talented chef in our house."

"Oh, please do tell her it's lovely." Hazel said.

"I will, Hazel, thank you. I'm sure she'll be delighted." He said and turned to continue his previous conversation with one of the boys.

Hazel looked around at the decorations that they had managed to put up already, it looked great so far. The autumn colours of the small flags swayed gently in the breeze. She was still looking around at the decorations when she spotted Rune, her cat, licking something off the main road. Rune then proceeded to lick her paws and clean her face as if she had found something very sticky and tasty. "I'll be right back." Hazel said to Rowan as she put her drink down. In a glance, she realised that Rowan and Drake were laughing so loud that they didn't hear her and she smiled to herself as she moved away.

Hazel walked back towards the empty road and Rune, trying to work out what the cat was licking on the road. As she got closer, she saw it was a dead mouse that had been squashed recently, probably by a passing car. "Eww...Rune, that's gross." As she walked out onto the road she felt in her back pocket for a tissue, she wanted to pick up the pieces of the mouse and take it off the road to bury it. Rune just looked up at her and tilted her head on one side as she approached.

Hazel knelt down and began picking up the pieces with the tissue whilst trying not to touch any of the bloody bits. She had to push Rune off who just wanted to carry on licking and chewing on the body. Hazel heard shouting behind her, presumed every on the green was having fun and carried on picking up the bits of the corpse.

Suddenly, she heard a high-pitched scream that sounded somehow wrong to her, somehow mechanical. She looked round to her right, but could see nothing unusual except it seemed to take ages for her vision to rotate round while the horrible screaming continued. She finally turned her head to the left.

Her vision was completely filled by a huge truck.

All she could see was its massive grill as it served away from her, just missing her by inches. The moment of joy she felt at knowing it had missed her faded very quickly when she saw it heading straight towards Rowan who was running towards her, waving her hands and shouting. Hazel realised that the screaming had been the tyres squealing on the road as the driver tried to break and because of that noise she had not heard Rowan's shouts.

Hazel watched helplessly as the truck closed in on Rowan. It skidded on the grass, the brakes doing absolutely nothing. She watched, horrified, as her brother Drake seem to run inhumanly fast, grab Rowan, swing her round and throw her away from the oncoming truck. Behind them the boys and Elder Furze scattered in all directions away from the old oak as the truck thundered towards them.

Everything had slowed down in Hazel's vision, like it was a scene from a slow motion action movie.

Drake was unable to get out of the way completely, he was caught by the front of the truck and flipped up into the air, disappearing behind the truck as it hit the old tree and came to an abrupt stop.

"Drake!" Hazel screamed, as everything returned to normal speed around her. She hauled herself up from the road and somewhere in her brain she realised that Rune had vanished, probably ran away in fright. Hazel looked toward the village green, the old tree was still shaking, dropping loose leaves and twigs but the driver had managed to slow down enough to not have snapped the tree in half. The front of the truck was damaged but Hazel was more worried about her brother, whom she still couldn't see.

She ran across the road and around the truck not knowing what she would find. Drake was laid on the ground, seemingly asleep, one arm was at such a strange angle that Hazel couldn't make sense of it, it was almost like he had two elbows in one arm. Elder Furze was kneeling next to Drake feeling in his neck for a pulse when Hazel ran to his side.

"Is he....?" She whispered but couldn't finish the sentence. She was scared of what the reply would be as she looked down at her brother's still and lifeless form.

Before she got any answer, chaos broke out as villagers from all directions ran onto the green shouting. The other boys staggered back and sat on the ground again, stunned. Rowan, her t-shirt covered in dirt and grass stains was holding her left wrist against her. She walked over and sat down next to Hazel, looking just as pale as Drake. Hazel eyes flicked to Rowan, her wrist then back to her brother. She was unable to speak, her mind was having trouble sorting out what had happened.

Time was still being strange as, in what seemed like only seconds, an ambulance arrived and two men in uniform jumped out. They asked everyone to step back from Drake so they could work. One of the men questioned Elder Furze about what happened, until the second called for his help to work on Drake. Drake was still very pale and seemed not to be breathing. The men called to him, one man rubbed his knuckles hard the top of Drake's chest just below the throat. Drake's eyes fluttered and opened slowly, like he had been in a deep sleep.

Hazel dropped to her knees and leaned over him, "Drake?"

"Please miss, stay back." The ambulance man said.

Another ambulance arrived with a police car, the ambulance men jumped out and after a quick check with the first team, they headed over to the truck driver who had managed to stagger out of his truck and was sat leaning against one of it's large wheels, holding a handkerchief to a cut on his forehead.

The policeman also questioned Elder Furze and the other boys.

The first ambulance man grabbed an oxygen mask and placed it over Drake's nose and mouth then put a drip into his undamaged arm. Together, the two men carefully placed his injured arm in an inflatable sleeve and placed him on a stretcher. One of the men caught sight of Rowan holding her wrist and went to have a look at it. It was quickly decided that it was probably broken and she too was placed in the first ambulance with Drake, within moments they were driving off quickly with the sirens going.

Hazel watched the first and then the second ambulance leave in a dream and all of a sudden she realised that her brother, her best friend and the truck driver were all hurt because of her, because she was stupid enough to walk out onto a road without looking and then kneel there messing with her cat and a dead mouse. Hazel burst into tears and sat sobbing on the grass.

She felt someone put their arms around her and hold her tight. It took a long time before she could stop crying, but eventually, gasping and hiccupping, she looked up into the kind eyes of Elder Daisy who still held her in her arms.

"Everything will be alright, Hazel. I promise." She said, in her calm gentle voice.

"But I...I...killed my brother." Hazel sobbed again and fell back against Elder Daisy's chest.

"No you haven't, love. He is conscious and it looks like he has a broken arm, maybe a few broken ribs but he is most certainly not dead, Hazel. Do you hear me? Hazel? Drake is alive and will mend, you'll see." She said.

Hazel pulled away and looked into Elder Daisy's honest eyes. Her kind face was very reassuring. Daisy was a small, round woman with thick shoulder length, silver hair. Her pale blue eyes were at the same level as Hazel's.

"Really? He's not..." Hazel said.

"Yes, really." She smiled and wiped the tears off Hazel's cheeks, "I said we'd meet your mum at the hospital. Elder Bear went to tell her and take her there as soon as he heard. We had best get going, I'm sure your mum is worried about you too."

Elder Daisy helped her up. Hazel was very wobbly legged so Daisy helped her walk across the street to her own cottage, beside the bakers, and helped her climb into her car. Within minutes they were driving down the main road on the way to the hospital.

"Thank the Gods you're alright." Hazel's mum, Pearl, said as she grabbed Hazel and hugged her tightly in the hospital corridor.

"I'm fine mum, what about Drake?" Hazel asked and looked around for her dad, "Where's dad?"

"Your brother is in with the doctor now and your dad's on his way back from work, he should be here soon. What happened? Are you sure you're okay?"

"Yes." Tears began to run down Hazels face again, "It was my fault, mum. I'm sorry, I was messing about in the road without looking and...and everyone got hurt because of it." Hazel hung her head, tears silently tumbling down her face and dripping onto the hospital floor.

"Oh love." Pearl enveloped her in the type of hug only a mum can give.

"What about, Roo?" Hazel suddenly remembered her friend.

"She is fine, Elder Bear has taken her to the x-ray department, they think her wrist is broken but she's fine apart from that."

Hazel's dad, Buck, arrived looking flustered, hot and very worried, just as the doctor came out of the examination room. Pearl and Buck talked with him while Elder Daisy took Hazel to sit on chairs in the nearby seating area. Hazel fiddled nervously with the material of her t-shirt.

Elder Daisy placed her hand over Hazel's hands, stilling them, "It will be alright, you'll see. " She said her hand remained holding Hazel's.

Hazel saw her parents shake hands with the doctor, they watched him walk away and turned to hug each other. Hazel's heart sank as they began to walk towards her, she tried to swallow but her mouth had dried up.

"Don't look so worried, my little nut. Drake is going to be fine." Her dad, Buck, said as he swept her up in his strong arms and held her.

"Thank the Gods." Exclaimed Elder Daisy, "What a relief."

Pearl hugged Daisy, "Oh yes, we are blessed." Pearl sat down heavily next to Daisy, "He has a broken arm and two broken ribs, they want to keep him in overnight for observation in case of concussion but then, hopefully, he will be able to come home. Although, he will be in plaster, of course, for a few weeks."

"Can I see him?" Hazel said.

"Of course you can, Nut. Let's you and me go and say hello, whatcha say?" Buck led Hazel by the hand to her brother's room.

Drake lay on top of the hospital bed in a hideous pale green hospital gown with his eyes shut, he looked pale and tired. His newly plastered right arm lay resting on a white pillow. He had a graze on his cheekbone that was beginning to swell under his eye, there were several other grazes on his other elbow and hand. His left shin looked bruised and had a large lump.

Hazel stood horrified at the end of the bed.

"Drake, it's dad. How are you son?" Buck said reaching his hand out to gently touch Drake's pale forehead.

Drake eyes opened and he smiled feebly, "I feel like I've been hit by a truck." He said as he began to laugh, then winced at the pain in his ribs.

Buck laughed heartily, "I can see ya not dead then."

Hazel looked in horror at her dad.

"Nope, need a bigger truck next time." Drake grinned. "Why ya hiding over there, sis? And why do you look like you've seen a ghost?"

"I...I thought you were dead." She said.

"Nice try but ya not getting my bacon yet." He joked.

Hazel balled her fists in frustration. Did he not know how close he had come to dying? "That's not funny!" Hazel shouted.

Her dad reached out and pulled her close, "Hey, he's okay, Nut. You can relax now, everything will be okay, and he'll heal."

"Hey, sis, I'm alright really. A bit bruised but still here." He smiled, tried to move his position but winced and gave up. Instead, he held his hand out to her.

Hazel took it in hers greedily, she loved her brother dearly even if he annoyed all the time. "I'm sorry. It was all my fault."

"Yes, it was...can I ask a favour?"

"Yes, anything."

"Can you be more careful from now on? I mean, can you look when you cross the road like any normal person because I don't want to get run over again." He grinned at her and winked.

"Oh Drake, I'm so sorry."

"S'okay, sis. Anyway the Doc said I could go home tomorrow if I don't throw up or pass out."

"That is very good news, son." Buck said.

"Anyone heard about Rowan, yet?" Drake asked, looking more worried for her than himself.

"Elder Daisy said she was fine and Elder Bear has gone with her for the x-ray, they think her wrist is broken." Hazel said.

"Thank the Gods she is okay." Drake said his whole body seemed to relax at the news.

"You probably saved her life, you know, Drake. I'm very proud of you, even if you could have gotten yourself killed in the process." Buck said.

"Thanks, dad. I didn't even think about it, I just did it when I saw the truck swerve from Hazel towards Rowan, I was already up running towards Hazel. It was just lucky I was there." He said and blushed.

"I knew you liked Roo." Hazel exclaimed.

"Shut up, Hazel." He snapped.

The door opened and Pearl walked in, "I heard shouting. What's going on?"

"Oh nothing out of the ordinary, dear. Everything is back to normal." Buck chuckled and put his arm around Pearl as Hazel and Drake glared at each other.

Drake did indeed return home the next day with an all clear for concussion and an appointment for another x-ray the following week, to see if the bones in his arm were healing correctly.

It is traditional in Brew, to celebrate Harvest Home by having a ritual up within the circle of thirteen stones on the Goddess Mound. The stones had been upon the mound for as long as anyone could remember and most of the 'turning of the wheel' seasonal celebrations were held there.

The large crowd had gathered as usual at the top of the Goddess Mound. Everyone knew their places, the Elders were stood within the ring of stones, one in front of each stone and the fire keeper tending the fire in the centre. The rest of the village stood outside the ring of stones forming a circle around them.

Hazel glanced at her brother to her left, he was stood next to his parents and awaiting the start of the ritual like everyone else. Drakes arm was plastered from wrist to elbow and covered in hand written get well messages, pictures and signatures from all his friends and family. He no longer wore the sling the hospital had given him in the beginning, the bruising on his face had developed into a marbled landscape of various shades of purple around his cheek bone and eye and, although no outward sign could be seen, Hazel knew that his broken ribs were bandaged tightly under his clothes.

Rowan stood at Drakes side, the pair had been inseparable since the accident just four days ago. Rowan's wrist had indeed been broken and she also had a plaster on it and, although smaller than Drakes, her plaster was also covered in get-well graffiti.

The ritual began with the local band, Moon Scape, playing the Harvest Home song, the Elders began to sing and the villages soon joined in.

Come ye thankful people come,
Raise the song of Harvest Home!
All is safely gathered in,
Ere the winter storms begin;
Goddess our Mother, doth provide
For our wants to be supplied:
Come to the Goddess's own temple, come,
Raise the song of Harvest Home.

All the world is the Goddess's own field
Fruit unto her praise to yield;

Wheat and tares together sown
Unto joy or sorrow grown;
First the blade, and then the ear,
Then the full corn shall appear;
Lady of the harvest grant that we
Wholesome grain and strong may be.

For our Goddess shall come,
And shall take her Harvest Home;
From her field shall in that day
All offences purge away,
Give her will charge at last
In the fire the stalks to cast;
But the fruitful ears to store
In her garner evermore.

Even so, Lady, quickly come,
Bring thy final Harvest Home;
Gather thou thy people of grain,
Free from sorrow, free from pain,
There, forever purified,
in thy presence to abide;
Come, with all the harvest, come,
Raise the glorious Harvest Home. [1]

As Elders Bear and Daisy began the blessings of the harvest
and the offerings to the Earth Mother, Hazels mind and eyes
wandered back to her Brother and her best friend. The deep
disappointment of knowing she was to blame for their pain hit
Hazel once again and she hung her head in shame.

The ritual moved onwards seemingly around Hazel as she
remained distracted, lost in her own mind reliving the acci-

dent. Seeing, once again, herself knelt down talking to Rune as the huge truck headed towards her and then ran off the road towards her brother and best friend. Hazel shuddered and opened her tired eyes. She had not had a proper nights sleep since the accident, she kept waking up after having nightmares about trucks crushing everyone she loved. Hazel's head felt woolly and heavy with lack of sleep and from worry and sadness over the accident.

Elder Bear's voice finally broke through into Hazel's tired mind, "It is now time for anyone who wants to make an offering of the harvest to the flames of our ancestors, before we close this ritual and proceed to the feasting on the village green."

A cheer went up as the villagers began approaching the fire in family groups, couples or singularly, placing gifts made of weaved corn leaves, corn dolls, seeds, nuts, dried leaves, paintings of the harvest and homemade crafts into the flames. Everyone cheered as each of the offerings burst into flame. The villagers were making sacrifices for a prosperous harvest next year, now that this year's harvest was complete. Some of the village children squealed with delight when their family's offerings burst into flame.

Hazel lingered at the back of the line with Drake, Rowan and her parents, who had thought it wise to go last so that Drake wouldn't get bumped about more than necessary by the passing people. When it finally became their turn, they walked up to the fire in the centre of the circle together. Hazel's mum and dad placed their offering of a homemade bread loaf into the large fire and a cheer went up from the other villagers as it burned. Rowan stepped forward and placed a bracelet she had made out of acorns into the flames, another cheer went up. Drake approached and dropped into the flames his sling and the crowd cheered loudly.

Hazel was the last to stand before the flames and before she revealed what her offering would be, she turned around to face Elder Bear and nodded once.

"Brothers and Sisters, if I could have your attention once again, please?" He said to the crowd.

Utter silence befell the circle of stones.

"Hazel would like to address you all." Elder Bear placed a reassuring hand on Hazel's shoulder and smiled encouragingly at her.

There were surprised murmurs in the crowd, Hazel's family and friends look startled. They had no idea she had intended to speak during the ritual.

Hazel's heart missed a beat and her breath came quickly. She took a deep breath and slowly breathed it out steadying herself. "Thank you, Elder Bear, for letting me talk to everyone." Hazel voice trembled slightly but she was determined to say what she wanted to say, she pulled out a piece of paper from the jeans pocket and turned to face the villagers, "My offering to the fire of our ancestors this year, is a picture I have drawn. It's not an ordinary picture of the harvest, it's a picture of all the reckless and stupid things I do, like crossing a road without looking and sitting talking to my cat in the middle of a road when a truck is trying to drive down it. Also, not using my helmet when I ride my bike and lot's of other things." She blushed to the roots of her curls.

Hazel glanced nervously at her family across the sacred circle. Her mum put her hand over her mouth and looked like she was about to cry.

"Recently, with what happened with the truck and Drake and Rowan getting hurt, I've realised that the things I do don't just affect me but also the people I love."

Hazel blushed again as she felt the eyes of the entire village upon her, she paused as she watched some of the villagers look over towards her family and Drake and Rowan and then look back at her expectantly.

"I could not stand it if anyone had died and I now understand that I need to be more sensible for myself and others. With this harvest I now truly understand what it means to 'reap what you sow' and I now burn my picture as a promise that from now onwards I will be a little more wise in my choices and a lot more careful about my own safety and that of the people around me." Hazel opened the folded piece of paper and reached over and placed it in the flames.

The villager's cheers rang out as they roared with approval of her words and deed. Elder's Bear and Daisy hugged Hazel, smiled and congratulated her on such an important step forward and as Hazel timidly returned to her family, they hugged her tightly and Hazel saw that her mother was indeed crying.

"I'm so proud of you." Mum said as she wiped away her happy tears.

"Well done, Nut. Well done." Her father said proudly.

Rowan hugged Hazel and whispered in her ear "Wow, that was brave. Good for you."

"Thanks." Hazel said.

"Does this mean I get your bacon now?" Drake said and winked.

"No!" Hazel burst out laughing, "But it does mean that I'll try not to get you run over by a truck again."

"Glad to hear it. It's not something I would like to repeat, thanks." He squinted his eyes as he peered at her, "Hmm...."

"What?"

"You realise I can't call you 'Hazel the Unwise' now, don't you?"

"Oh, that's a shame." Sarcasm dripped from every word.

"I'm gonna have to think up a new name for you. How about 'Hazel the Cautious' or 'Hazel the Safety Girl' or how about 'Hazel the Wise'?" He grinned evilly.

"Mum!?"

---

[1] *Original lyrics of 'Come, Ye Thankful People Come' by Sir George J. Elvey (1816 - 1893). Pagan related lyrics added by Edain Duguay 2010.*

Yew the Bored Witch

An Introduction to Yew

Each of the children of Brew have been named after things in Nature and Yew is no exception.

Named after the Yew tree, which is sometimes regarded as the most sacred tree to the druids with its symbolism of death and rebirth, due to the fact that the outer tree dies and a new tree grows within. It represents transformation and reincarnation and may be used to enhance magical/psychic abilities as well as induce vision.

Yew is twelve years old, very clever and gets bored quickly. She is small, with short spiky blond hair and glasses. She has been living with her Grandma since her parents died in a car crash when she was seven years old. Her Grandma is, understandably, rather over protective of Yew and tends to do everything for her without realising she is spoiling her.

Our tale begins a week before Samhain, otherwise known as the Celtic or seasonal New Year. This is a time of year when the veil between this world and the ghostly realm is the thinnest. It is a time to remember lost loved ones and the ancestors.

Yew the Bored Witch

Yew peeked out from under the blanket as Grandma approached the sofa with a steaming mug of 'herbal delight'. That's what Grandma called it, but Yew knew it tasted horrible and decided her Grandma must never have tasted it. Taking the mug she sipped the tea, trying really hard not to let the hideous taste show on her face. After a few sips, her Grandma took the mug from her and placed it happily on the side table.

Yew snuggled deeper into the double thickness of her Grandmas multi-coloured knitted blanket until just her spiky hair and her glasses, which framed her grey eyes, showed.

"Are you feeling any better, dear?" Grandma said as she placed her soft, wrinkled hand on Yew's forehead to check her temperature. Blossom, Yew's Grandma, is a small, round lady with a happy wrinkled face. She has a gentle and soft voice and long, thick white hair.

"About the same." Yew said.

"You'll be better in no time, once you finish the tea." Grandma smiled sweetly down at her.

"Hmmm..." Yew said doubtfully. "I'm bored."

"Why don't you read, dear? I could fetch you a book or perhaps we could watch a movie?"

"A book maybe, I'm bored of all our movies." Yew said with a sigh.

"Shall I fetch the one by your bed?"

"Yes, thanks Gran. That would be great." Yew perked up and realised she may look too well and Gran might not believe her and not give her a note for school. There was no way she was going to school today. It was sports day and Yew found sports utterly boring.

Grandma headed for the stairs and started the climb to Yew's room in the attic of their small cottage. Meanwhile, Yew lay gazing out of the patio door, opposite the sofa, into the garden. The garden looked dead with all the bushes losing their leaves and the plants slowly withering away in the middle of October. The twilight made it seem even more dead and uninviting.

Unseen by Yew, her Grandma's ascent was a difficult one. By the time she had arrived in the attic, she was out of breath and her bad hip was hurting her. She paused for a moment and took a deep breath, gently blowing it out while her heart calmed down. She gritted her teeth against the pain in her hip as she crossed the small room for Yew's book, taking care to mind the low beams.

Once again, Blossom braced herself, this time for the downstairs trip. Slowly, but surely, she managed it but going down was a lot harder than going up. Thank goodness her bedroom was on the ground floor, she thought. Taking another steadying breath, she made her way back to the sofa giving Yew her reading book.

"Here you are, dear." Grandma said with a smile to hide the pain.

"Thanks, Gran." Yew took the book, opened it at her marker and without looking up, asked, "What's for dinner?"

"Chicken pie. I'm going to use the left over chicken from yesterday." She said as she turned heading to the kitchen, "You must be feeling better if you're hungry." She called over her shoulder.

Yew didn't answer for fear of giving herself away and settled to read her book while her Gran began to cook dinner.

In the small rustic kitchen, Grandma collected all her ingredients and pulled her high stool over to the counter. She sat with a pleasurable sigh, the pain in her hip lessening. She reached out for her pills on the narrow shelf in front of her and took two, noticing that there weren't many left. She made a mental note to make a doctors appointment tomorrow.

The following day, Yew decided she would make a full recovery, explaining it as a twenty-four hour bug and return to school as normal. Her Grandma dropped her off at school, as usual and went off to do errands. Yew liked school on Fridays, her day consisted of maths, science and computer studies, all the subjects she loved and did well at, sometimes they were so easy she even got bored in class and had time to read further on in the text books making her way ahead of the other students.

Yew sat with her friend Ivy in the final lesson of the day. The Math equations were too easy again and Yew had finished them well ahead of the rest of class. Instead of reading the next lesson in her book, she sat gazing out the window into the small garden courtyard of the school. The shrubs and trees were dropping their leaves as Yew watched the cool autumn breeze make them flutter to the ground silently.

Yew didn't like autumn, she didn't like that everything began to die, and it reminded her that it was the time of year her parents had died five years ago. She would be happy when autumn was over and the winter snow had arrived. Yew loved the snow, she felt it made everything look bright and clean. It masked all the dead looking plants and trees, making them look beautiful and new again.

"Hey! Wake up the bell just rang." Ivy nudged her, "Time to enjoy the weekend!"

Yew's head spun around startled by her friend's words. Ivy's brilliant green eyes stared into Yew's.

"What planet are you on?" Ivy said as she stood, collected her books and stuffed them in her backpack.

"I didn't hear the bell." Yew mentally shook herself and looked around at everyone leaving the classroom.

"I noticed. You okay?" Ivy flicked her long, dark braid back over her slim shoulder.

"Yeah. Let's get out of here." Yew packed up her books and left for home.

The girls walked a few blocks and then separate at the village green.

By the time Yew arrived at her front door, the sky was full of dark ominous clouds. "I'm home, Gran!" She called as she closed their front door behind her and hung up her coat.

"I'm in the kitchen. How was your day, love?" Gran called.

Yew grabbed her backpack and headed for the sofa, where she sat heavily, throwing her bag next to her. "It was okay. Looks like we're getting a storm, it's getting really dark out there."

Gran came in drying her hands on a towel, which she threw over her shoulder to keep it handy. "Yes, the weather man on the radio said a cold front was heading this way and we are to expect a lot of rain." Glancing at the dark sky out of the patio doors, Gran limped across the living room and closed the heavy curtains. "There, that's better."

"How's your hip?" Yew said as she dragged out her school books to sort the ones that needed homework doing.

"Just the same dear, thanks." Gran bravely smiled and headed back towards the kitchen. "Dinner will be in half an hour and I was just about to make some tea. Would you like a cup?"

"Yes, please." Yew said as she opened her computer science textbook and began to read it. She liked to get her homework over with, straight after school, and especially on a Friday so she could have the whole weekend to herself.

Yew had managed to complete her homework in time for bed that night. She lay in her warm thick covers and read by the lamplight until her eyelids drooped and she kept reading the same sentence over and over. She decided it was time to sleep. She snuggled down, switch off the light and drifted off into a peaceful sleep. Her sleep became disturbed as she tossed and turned in her bed, the dream became more strange and disjointed until it eventually cleared and she was left with a single image.

The image of her parents trying to tell her something.

Her dead parents.

Yew was startled awake by the dream. She lay blinking in the early morning light, trying to grasp at the whispery tendrils of her dream as it faded away. Her parents had been stood by an old dying tree on a cold grey day, they both wore dark brown cloaks or robes and had been desperately talking to her but Yew could hear no sounds coming from their mouths. Her mother had held out her hand to Yew, it contained something small but she had awoken before she could see what it was. The dream hadn't been frightening but it had an urgent feel to it, as if what they were trying to tell her was important somehow.

She had often dreamt of her parents but this had been the first time they had tried to tell her something. Usually Yew saw them walking together through fields, in all different weathers and in all seasons, they were always holding hands. Yew took a deep breath as she felt the familiar ache inside her chest for her long dead parents and snuggled back down into the warmth of her bed. Her mind tiredly tried to go back over the dream again and again until she finally drifted off into an exhausted sleep.

The light through Yew's eyelids seemed too bright, she blinked them open, happily remembering it was Saturday. The light in her room seemed odd still, perhaps she was coming down with a bug, after all it would serve her right for faking it on Thursday to miss sports day. Yew climbed out of bed, walked across the creaky floorboards and peaked out of her curtains, to her surprised everything was white and glowing in the bright morning's sunshine. She blinked several times as her eyes adjusted to the brightness.

"Yew? Are you awake? You will never guess what has happened." Grandma called up the stairs.

"It snowed." Yew said as she grabbed her dressing gown and ran down the stairs. She gave her Grandma a big excited hug as she rushed to the patio window in the lounge. All the dead or dying plants and bare trees were covered in several inches of pure new snow. The garden looked like something from a fairytale and Yew loved it.

"So much for the rain they promised." Gran said as she peered over Yew's shoulder.

"Oh, but this is so much better." Yew said.

Yew quickly washed and dressed, she gobbled down her breakfast in her rush to get outside and meet her friends. She couldn't wait to have fun in the snow.

"You be careful outside." Gran said, "I'm off to Daisy's this morning, there's a meeting about the Samhain celebration next weekend. I'll be back for lunch though, so make sure you are."

"Okay." Yew said as she flew out the front door. Closing it quickly behind her. She suddenly stopped and looked down at the path that led from their front door to the garden gate and the road. It was white and perfect, not one mark on it. Yew loved this part of any snowfall, the chance to be the first person to ever stand on it.

Yew gingerly placed her right foot down on the snow, it made a satisfying crunching noise as she put her weight on it and then she carefully placed her left foot down one step ahead, again another wonderful crunch. She took two more careful steps then glanced behind her and saw her foot depressions in the perfect snow.

She giggled to herself as she walked down to the garden gate and looked back. Her single trail in the snow felt somehow exciting and yet comforting but she didn't have any more time to waste and rushed off to get her friends Ivy and Holly out to play in it.

By lunchtime, Yew was tired and wet from the melting ice. She had spent several hours with a large group of her friends-- Ivy, Holly, Birch, Ash, Rowan, Willow and Hazel--throwing snow balls and making snowmen on the village green. There were many children out playing in the snow, some parents had brought out sledges and were dragging their children around, all of them were enjoying this early snowfall while it lasted.

As the friends split to go back to their respective homes for lunch, Yew made her way back to hers looking forward to lunch, hoping it would be some of her grandma's warming soup. She walked back up their path to the front door but found it locked, perhaps her Grandma was still at the meeting she thought and dug her key out of her jeans pocket. She let herself inside just as the phone rang. Quickly kicking of her snow covered wet boots, Yew ran for the phone almost slipping on the wooden floor in her socks as she rushed.

"Hello?" Yew said.

"Ah, there you are Yew." Said Elder Daisy, Yew's great aunt and her Grandma's sister.

"Hello Aunt Daisy." Yew smiled into the phone when she recognised the voice. "Is Gran still with you? Can you tell her I've come home for lunch like she asked?" She said and she began, with one hand, to unzip her hoody and struggle out of it without dropping the phone.

"It's about your Gran, she was just leaving here when she had a terrible fall with her bad hip."

Yews heart sank with fear, "What? Is she alright? Shall I come over?"

"The ambulance has just taken her to the hospital, they think she may have broken her hip. I'll be over in a few minutes and we can both go to the hospital. Okay?"

"Okay."

"Don't worry, love. Everything will be alright. I'll be there in a minute." Daisy said as she hung up.

Yew was stood half in and half out of her hoody staring at the phone. Her mind was not working with the sudden shock of the news. Yew had the urge to sit down and managed the few steps to the nearest chair where she sat heavily, phone still in hand. For a few moments she stared into space her brain not thinking and then a horrid thought struck her. What if Gran wasn't alright? What if Aunt Daisy was just saying that to not make her worry?

Terror gripped Yew as she realised that she could not lose her Gran, it had been bad enough losing her parents even all those years ago but her Gran was her world now. What would she do without her? Yew's brain finally kicked back into gear and began to rationalize her thoughts. Her Gran may have broken her hip but that is not life threatening, she would be okay.

Yew took a deep breath and then another and forced herself to move. She place the phone back on it's charger and pulled her hoody back on, zipping it up as she slipped her feet back into her winter boots. Just as she grabbed her coat, there was a knock at the door and in walked Aunt Daisy. Before Yew knew what was happening she was in the strong warm embrace of her aunt.

Daisy is almost a perfect copy of Yew's Grandma, she is also a small curvy lady with one of those faces that never stops smiling, she always made everyone feel happy and relaxed and, because of this, many came to her for advice. She also has shoulder length thick, wavy grey hair but has blue eyes instead of Grey like Yew's Grandma has.

Within moments of the comforting hug, Daisy had got Yew out of the house and into her car heading towards the hospital. The journey to the hospital took about twenty minutes and was a very quiet one. Both Yew and Daisy were lost in their own thoughts and concerns about Blossom.

As they entered the hospital, the snow was already beginning to melt under the warm autumn sunshine. Melted ice dripped of the entrance canopy and the snow on the path outside had become slushy. They stamped off the ice from their boots on the mat and went to find out where Blossom was. They were told that she was in with a doctor at the moment and that they would have to wait in the waiting room. They would send the doctor into to see them when he had finished his assessment.

Time slowly ticked by as Yew and Daisy sat in the empty waiting room designed for the patient's family. There were twelve cream coloured chairs around the walls, two coffee tables covered with magazines, a small box of toys, a water cooler and a TV fastened high up on one wall. The TV was tuned to a 24 hr cooking channel and the sound turned off but the subtitles switched on. The room was very bland and way too bright.

Yew fiddled with her nails. She tried looking at the magazines but just got bored and so gave up. How much longer will the doctor be? She wondered to herself for the hundredth time. She wanted to see her Grandma now, she wanted to know she was safe.

At last, the door of the waiting room opened and a tall, slim doctor with greying hair walked in. "I'm looking for the family of Blossom...."

"Yes!" Yew said as she jumped to her feet.

The doctor looked at Yew and then at Daisy.

Daisy stood, "I'm her sister, Daisy, and this is her Granddaughter, Yew."

"I'm Doctor Tamarack, please have a seat." He gestured to them both as he perched on the edge of the coffee table in front of them.

Yew and Daisy looked at him expectantly.

"I can confirm that Blossom has a Femoral Neck fracture...she has broken her hip and due to the severe arthritis in the joint, she is going to need surgery. She needs an arthroplasty...a total hip replacement."

"Oh." Daisy said.

"What does that mean?" Yew looked at Daisy.

"It means...this procedure involves replacing part of your Grandma's thigh bone and the socket in her pelvic bone with prostheses." The doctor said.

"Will she be able to walk again?" Yew asked.

"Oh yes, love." Daisy smiled at her and put an arm around her comfortingly.

"Yes, she will, but it will take a lot of hard work and she will need a lot of help. She won't be able to get around like she used to for several months. Do you think you can help her?" The doctor smiled kindly at her.

"Yes." Yew said confidently, glad to know she would be able to help her Gran in the months to come.

"Good, she will need you both very much when she gets home but we can talk about all that after the operation. She's scheduled to be operated on soon, we're just waiting for the anaesthetist to arrive. This early snowstorm is making the roads very difficult."

"When can she come home?" Daisy said.

"If there are no complications from the surgery, probably Thursday."

"Five days?" Yew said.

"Yes, a hip fracture is a serious injury and we like to keep the patient in for a minimum of five days. It is not like breaking an arm, where we can patch you up and let you go."

"We understand, Doctor. Thank you." Daisy nodded at the doctor and held Yew's hand. "Do you need me to sign anything?"

"No, Blossom has done all that." He said.

"Can I see her?" Yew said.

"Yes, but for a very short time as she has been given very strong pain killers. I suggest you both check in on her and then go home."

Both Yew and Daisy were about to argue with his suggestion when he held a hand up.

"Your Grandma is due for surgery shortly and it will take several hours to perform, then she'll be in recovery and asleep for several hours after that, I think it's the best idea."

"Will you ring me if there is any problem? I gave reception my number."

Yew glanced worriedly at Daisy.

"Of course, but it will all go smoothly and you can see her tomorrow." He said confidently.

"Thank you, Doctor Tamarack." Daisy said.

"No problem." He said as he stood up, "Now let's go and see your Grandma, shall we?"

They followed the doctor down several corridors to a small private room where he opened the door and followed them in. The room was a pale green colour with a huge window and vertical blinds with Gran's bed in the centre against the left hand wall. She was asleep and looked pale, with her white hair fanning out on the white hospital pillow. There was an IV drip going into her left arm.

"Gran?" Yew said softly as she moved nearer the bed and gently held her hand. Yew looked at Daisy, her eyes widening with worry and alarm.

"The pain medication is making her sleepy." Doctor Tamarack said.

"Blossom, can you hear me?" Daisy said as she came to stand by Yew.

Blossom's eyes fluttered open and she frowned for a few moments while her eyesight cleared. "Yew? Daisy?" Blossom sounded panicked.

"Shhh...love, yes we're here. Everything is going to be alright." Daisy said.

"Oh Gran, are you okay?" Yew said.

Blossom nodded slowly, her eyes were beginning to close again.

"I'm sorry ladies, but Blossom needs to rest." Doctor Tamarack said.

"Of course." Daisy said to him and turned back to her sister, "Don't worry about anything, sis. I'll stay with Yew, you just get better." She patted her sister's arm and began to move away.

"I'll be back tomorrow Gran...I love you." Yew said as the tears began to tumble down her cheeks.

Blossom looked peaceful as she floated back off to sleep not seeing her sister wipe away Yew's tears and cuddle her as they left the room.

Daisy took Yew home and, after collecting a few belongings, she stayed with Yew at Blossoms house in the spare room. The following morning Yew and Daisy were back at the hospital visiting Blossom just in time to see Doctor Tamarack as he completed his rounds. After a brief discussion with the Doctor, Daisy and Yew entered Blossom's room.

"Gran!" Yew said as she rushed to the bed relieved to see her Grandma awake and looking less pale than then yesterday. "How are you?" She stood by the bed holding her Gran's hand.

Daisy pulled up a chair and sat. "Blossom, how are you?"

"I'm alright, I'm alright. Don't you fuss now." Blossom said in her usual no nonsense voice.

Yew burst into tears, so happy was she that her Gran was herself again.

"Yew, love, I'm alright." She patted Yew's hand, "How about giving your old Gran a kiss?" She smiled at her granddaughter.

Yew leaned in and gently hugged and kissed her Gran on her soft cheek. "Does it hurt?"

"Not really, it sort of aches but they do have me on strong pain killers though. It hurts more if I try to move." She said. "I'm glad to see you two. Are you looking after each other?"

"Don't you worry about us, sis. We are getting along just fine. I've put myself in your spare room so it's easier for Yew and she can still be at home while you are in here. Did they tell you how long you would be in?" Daisy said.

"Yes, the Doctor explained everything, what a lovely young man he is." Blossom said with a twinkle in her eye. "He was also talking about the rehabilitation exercises I need to start doing, once I get home. It seems it's going to take some time until I'm properly back on my feet. All because I lost my footing on the silly snow." Blossom sighed and shook her head.

"Not to worry Gran, we'll look after you. Won't we Aunt Daisy?" Yew beamed, feeling much happier now.

"Of course, we will." Daisy said.

"That nice Doctor said that a nurse would visit me at home to check on my progress and check the stitches. Apparently, they want to get me moving today, can you believe it? The wonders of modern medicine." Blossom smiled at them both.

"Today?" Daisy said.

"Wow, Gran. That's fast."

"Is that normal? I mean he was only telling us yesterday that it was a serious injury." Daisy looked shocked.

"Yes, that's what he said. Something to do with speedier recovery, he said someone will be assisting me with a walker and it will just be a few steps. He said I will be on pain killers and antibiotics for a while so it won't be too bad."

Yew and Daisy sat and spent time with Blossom for the rest of the visiting hours and made a list of things she needed for her stay in hospital, which they would bring back with them later that day. They returned home to find many bags and bouquets of flowers sat on the doorstep.

Yew peered inside the bags as she ferried them into the house, many were filled with home cooked meals and cookies, others with books, magazines, chocolates and cards for Blossom.

"Wow, look at all this." Yew said as she spread it all out on the kitchen counter.

"Our friends have been so generous, bless them." Daisy said as she peered at the cooked meals. "We can put one or two in the fridge and the rest in the freezer. This will keep us going until your Gran gets home and maybe even longer. Oh, Holly's mum's meat and vegetable stew with herb bread, now that is something to look forward to." She began moving the bowls and dishes to the freezer.

"Aunt Daisy?"

"Hmmm...?"

"I was wondering something..."

Daisy closed the freezer and turned to face Yew, "What is it, dear?"

"Gran won't be able to do much, will she? I mean when she gets home." Yew fiddled with the edge of her t-shirt as she looked at her aunt.

"No, not much at all. She will need help to dress and wash, even move about at first. She won't be able to clean up or stand here in her kitchen baking for hours like she used to, at least not for a few months."

"Poor Gran, won't she get bored?"

"Well, it's our job to see that she doesn't, right?" Daisy and hugged Yew, "Let's take it one day at a time, okay?"

"Okay." Yew nodded.

"Now you go and sort your Gran's things from her list while I heat up some stew and then we can go back and see her."

Over the next few days, Yew went to visit her Gran every evening after school, while Daisy went twice a day. So many of Blossom's friends visited her that her room was filled with flowers and get-well cards. Blossom had indeed taken her first few shaky steps and every day since she had managed more and more, until she could now get herself to the bathroom and back with the walker but still needed assistance to sit and stand.

On the Thursday morning, Yew awoke suddenly from yet another dream about her parents. It was almost the same as the last one; they were stood in front of an old dying tree on a cold grey day, they both wore dark brown cloaks or robes and her mother had held out her hand to Yew, it contained some-thing small, which she placed on the ground but Yew still couldn't see what it was.

Also, this time, they were not trying to tell her anything, they were looking directly at her and smiling, a huge wave of love and happiness came from them and wrapped Yew in the most wonderful and safe embrace. This feeling was so strong that it had woken her up and she lay in bed with a huge smile on her face and a heart full of love, it even brought happy tears to her eyes. She felt different somehow, changed by the dream by the knowledge of her parents love.

Yew with her happy heart waited on the doorstep to welcome her Grandma home from the hospital that afternoon. Everything had been prepared, from a higher chair in the living room to the raising of Gran's bed. The doctor had told Blossom to not raise her hip or bend more than 90 degrees and everything had been arranged with this in mind.

At last, Aunt Daisy's car pulled into the driveway on the chilly, late autumn afternoon. Taking their time, and with great care, Blossom and Daisy managed to get out of the car and inside the house, the door was finally closed against the cold onset of twilight.

Sitting by the roaring fire, Blossom, Daisy and Yew drank tea and ate peanut butter cookies especially made by Yew, as they are her Gran's favourites. Yew sat on a cushion by her Gran, as was their custom on cold nights when the fire was lit.

"It's good to be home." Blossom said.

"I bet it is." Daisy said.

"Welcome back, Gran." Yew said for the third time in the last half hour and beamed with happiness.

"These cookies are really good. Thanks, Daisy." Blossom smiled and took another off the plate.

"Oh I didn't make them." Daisy looking meaningfully at Yew.

"Don't tell me you made them, Yew?" Gran's face was the picture of surprise.

"Yes." Yew said proudly.

"She made them while I came to collect you, she is turning into a really good cook."

"Cooking and baking? Whatever next?" Gran said as she squeezed Yew shoulder with pride.

"You'll be surprised what she made me show her this last week."

"Oh?"

"I thought I had better learn some things around the house to help out seeing as you are hurt but also it's nice to be able to do things myself." Yew smiled shyly, blushing at her Gran.

"What a lovely thought. What else have you been learning?"

"Well, apart for the cooking and baking, Daisy has shown me how to clean everything and how the washer works, oh and Elder Heather has been over showing me some simple herbal teas to help you."

"Yew has taken her responsibilities very seriously and has been working very hard while you were away. I'm so proud of her." Daisy leaned back into the sofa with her mug smiling at her sister and great niece.

"I'm proud of you too. I know you will be a great help and think of all the fun we can have thinking up new recipes to try."

"That will be fun." Yew jumped up and kissed her Gran on the cheek.

Three days later, on the Sunday, it was Samhain and as normal in Brew, all Festival days were celebrated at the ancient stone circle on the Goddess Mound. The Samhain ritual is always held at night and once completed the entire village of Brew has a potluck feast. This year's hosts for the Samhain Feast were Elders Wolf and Violet who own a farm and the feast is to be in one of their barns.

Twilight came as Yew watched the villagers walk by her front garden heading towards the Goddess Mound. Her Gran knew that a way had been found so that she may attend the celebration, without having to walk up the spiralling path to the top but she didn't know how they were going to do it.

Yew, Daisy and Blossom were dressed in their warm clothes as it was a chilly night and extra blankets were brought out to keep Blossom warm. At last, their transport arrived, Elder Wolf pulled up on the road outside their cottage. Yew and Daisy helped Blossom walk slowly down to the gate with her walker.

"Oh my!" Blossom said as she saw her way up the mound.

Elder wolf had come with his small tractor, the type you use to cut large lawns and attached behind it was a small trailer. In the trailer was a high chair, similar to the one in Blossom's lounge, the chair was fastened to the trailer and it even had a canopy over it made from a large garden umbrella. The trailer had folding down steps, which Elder Wolf had just pulled down and secured in place.

"Heath Robinson would be proud, Wolf. What have you been up to?" Blossom laughed.

"Heard you might need a bit of help gettin' to ritual Blossom." Said Elder Wolf, a small man with a ruddy complexion and curly grey hair.

Without a second thought, he gently helped Blossom, steadying each of her steps until she was safely seated in the chair. The height of it made her head and shoulders above everyone else.

"Come along you two." He said to Daisy and Yew as he grabbed some cushions from behind the chair and put one on each wheel box inside the trailer, "Looks like you get a lift too." He grinned at them.

Yew climbed up and placed a blanket over Blossoms legs. "Are you comfy?"

"Yes, and a little embarrassed." Gran said.

"Just one last thing before we go..." Elder Wolf reached down by the chair and gave Gran one end of a seat belt, he reached down the other side and gave her the other end, "Don't want you falling out, do we?" He winked at Gran as he fastened it.

"Oh, Wolf you are clever." Blossom said.

"Get away with ya." He said as he stepped down and climbed back up in the driver's seat. "Good job I mow the mound all summer, I know where the potholes are and how to avoid them. Okay, here we go ladies. Blossom, you holler if you need to stop, alright?" With that he started the engine and pulled slowly and gently away from the curb.

The small tractor and its trailer made its way through the crowd with everyone waving and shouting hello to its riders. Slowly it wound its way down the lane that led to the mound, the crowd of walkers parted and it noisily made its way up the spiral path of the mound until it reached the top, luckily with only one or two bumps that made Blossom drawn in her breath sharply.

The circle of ancient stones reached up to the darkening sky like grey fingers reaching for the stars. In front of each of the stones was a lit torch, thirteen in total, which cast a warm glow all around. The villagers placed themselves between the stones but not in the circle, only the thirteen Elders, all clad in black robes, stood within.

Wolf drove the tractor around so that Blossom's chair was facing the centre of the stone circle, the lit firepit and the altar. They were even near enough to be able to feel some warm from the fire. Everyone thanked Wolf as he went to stand with his wife, also an Elder, in his place by a standing stone. Daisy stepped down and went to join Elder Bear at the Altar, as she is the Co-Leader of the Elders with him. They would be officiating this Samhain ritual, however, the Elders usually shared the responsibilities of the rituals and took turns officiating.

Yew huddled under a spare blanket close to her Grandma. "Are you okay?" She asked.

"Yes, thanks love. Those couple of bumps hurt a bit but the rest was fun." Gran smiled with excitement in her eyes. "That was so kind of Wolf, everyone has been so kind."

"That's because we all love you Gran." Yew said.

"I love you too, dear."

As the remainder of the villagers arrived at the stone circle, a hushed silence of anticipation fell over the crowd as they waited for the ritual to begin.

"Welcome everyone and Blessed Samhain." Elder Bear stepped forward and raised his arms.

Yew thought it made him look like a giant, as he is already a tall man. She liked Elder Bear, he had a deep voice, a kind happy face and a large beard.

"Blessed Samhain." The villagers called back as one.

"As you all know, Samhain is the end of the seasonal year and the beginning of a new one." He said.

Daisy stepped forward next to Elder Bear, "A time when we consider the seeds we planted and the fruit they bore over the last year. It is the season of death and rebirth, of life shed and renewal." She said.

"It's also a time when we decide what seeds we wish to plant in the soil of our lives and the result we hope to get." Elder Bear said. "At Samhain, we also greet and thank our Ancestors for their lives and actions, for their roles in our lives and be grateful for them."

"As is our custom, we welcome the God and Goddess to this rite." Daisy said as she lit two large candles on the altar.

"God and Goddess be with us." Bear said.

"Be with us." The villagers replied.

Daisy poured water into a large earthen bowl, which held a feather from a bird.

"Spirits of the Land, Sea and Sky be with us." Bear said.

"Be with us." The villagers replied.

Daisy poured a bottle of mead into the engraved ceremonial horn and poured a little into the flames of the fire pit.

"Ancestors be with us." Bear said.

"Be with us." The villagers replied.

"For those that wish to add a stone for a loved one that has passed away in this last year or to leave an offering on the Ancestor Cairn, please come forward." Daisy said.

Behind the altar, almost at the far side of the circle, the Ancestor Cairn sat glowing by torchlight. It was a pile of stones arranged in a mound shape, each stone representing a loved one. The piled stones made small holes and ledges were small candles and offerings were left.

The villagers, who wished to lay a stone or leave an offering, formed an orderly line at the side of the Ancestor Cairn while the local group, Moon Scape, who were placed just outside of the stone circle near the Ancestor Cairn, softly played a drum beat.

Yew withdrew the bag of seeds from her pocket, "Do you want me to place your offering for you Gran?"

"That would be very kind of you, love." Blossom reached into her jacket pocket and brought out a deep red apple, "Give your parents my love, will you?"

"Of course, Gran." Yew took the apple and kissed her Gran on the cheek. She climbed down of the trailer and joined the ever-moving line of people.

As Yew waited her turn she listened to the gentle drumbeats and watched as children and adults placed their stones, offerings or just simply touched the cairn and whispered words of love. She had done this every year since her parents had died but this was the first time she had done it for her Grandma and it somehow made her feel good inside.

Finally, her turn came. She stepped out from the queue of people into the empty quiet surrounding the Cairn. Going down on her knees, she looked for a place to put their offerings. Each ledge and hole was filled with acorns, mushrooms and apples also with tea lights, ribbons and coins. At last she found a small shelf, poured out the seeds and placed the apple next to them.

"Mum, Dad, these are for you. They are from Gran and I, Gran broke her hip so I'm doing this for her but don't worry I'll look after her. I've been learning a lot so I can help more and I think that would make you happy. I know you can see how well I'm doing. We love you and miss you very much." Yew brushed away a tear that had run down her cheek and stood. She took one last look at the Cairn and began, thoughtfully, to make her way back to her Grandma.

Yew watched from her seat on the trailer as the line to the Cairn continued until everyone had done what he or she needed to. During this time the Elders had filled several horns with the Ancestor mead and were passing it around the gathered villagers.

"Please take a drink of the blessed mead and raise the horn to our Ancestors." Bear said.

The drumbeat moved from a less sombre tune to an upbeat one as the horns were passed around the circle. Yew could hear various toasts to the Ancestors from the drinkers. At last, it was Yew and Blossoms turn, Elder Wolf had brought the horn over and passed it up to them. Yew passed it to her Gran without drinking, she was taught that the eldest of the family gets to toast the Ancestors first.

Gran took the horn and held it in the air for a few moments with her eyes shut. Yew presumed she was saying a private prayer or blessing. Blossom opened her eyes and took a small sip. "Oh that is lovely, I see Bear has been perfecting his mead recipe." She said.

Yew giggled and took the horn, she paused for a moment and said, "To our Ancestors because without them we wouldn't be here." She laughed and took a drink, "Hmmm...that is nice. It tastes like chocolate mead." She grinned as she passed the horn back down to Elder Wolf.

"I'll tell him you enjoyed it." He said and winked at her before going to the next group with the horn.

After several minutes, when everyone had raised the horn, the circle began to quieten again. The attention focused back onto Elders Bear and Daisy who were still stood in front of the Altar. The night was fully upon them now and their faces glowed in the torchlight.

"I would now like to call on those here that would like to say a few words about their Ancestors, their planted seeds for last year and their future plans for the coming year." Daisy held her hands out to the crowd, "Please come and share with us."

Yew and her Grandma watched as people stepped forward one by one and told their stories from the past year. Some remembered loved ones recently lost, others told of projects completed and plans laid for new ones. One couple announced that they would be Handfasted in the New Year, which made the crowd applaud and cheer loudly. Some stepped forward and told of new businesses started, while one admitted they had finally sorted out their garage as promised last year to another round of enthusiastic applause.

At one quiet point Blossom thrust her hand in the air to be heard, as she obviously couldn't step forward to speak.

"I believe Elder Blossom has something to say." Daisy informed everyone.

The entire village turned to look at Blossom and Yew found herself blushing for her Grandma.

"I just wanted to say thank you to everyone who has helped me since my fall, your kindly delivered meals, presents and cards, indeed even this trailer have shown just what wonderful and special people you all are. I especially want to thank my sister Daisy for everything and my Granddaughter Yew who has gone out of her way to become more self-sufficient as a way to help me." Gran's eyes filled with tears as she grabbed Yew's hand. "You are all very loved, thank you." She meant the comment for all but said it directly to Yew.

The crowd cheered and applauded again.

Yew meekly placed her hand in the air and caught Daisy's eye.

"Yes, Yew?"

Again the entire village turned their heads, this time their look was directed at her and she blushed furiously. She took a deep breath and let it out slowly just like her Gran had always taught her to do when nervous.

"May I say something?"

"Of course." Daisy said smiling.

Various people in the crowd called out encouraging words to show their agreement.

Yew stared at her shoes as she spoke, "As you all know my parents died five years ago this October and I have always hated this time of year. All the dead things...they remind me of...them. I've dreamed about Mum and Dad for as long as I can remember but last week they seemed to be trying to tell me something..." She glanced up and looked out at the sea of faces. She turned to look at her Gran who, once again, had tears in her eyes.

"Go on, love." Gran said quietly.

Yew lifted her head and looked back to the crowd, determined even if nervous. "I understand now what they were trying to say to me, to show me. They have always shown themselves in front of an oak tree, through the many seasons and that oak has grown, been full of leaves, the leaves have changed and it eventually died. This they have shown me over and over, until last week when mum tried to show me something in her hand. I have just realised what that was and what it all means." Yew paused and realised there was utter silence around the circle.

She swallowed hard and said, "Mum was trying to show me an acorn, just a simple beautiful acorn in her hand, she was bending to the ground to plant it. Plant the seed of life and I realised that's what they have been trying to say. That death is a part of life not separate from it. Everything alive must die at some point and it is not death we should fear. I think we should accept it, I should accept it and stop hating the reminders...like the death of the plants in autumn. They will grow back, just as life goes on for us and although my mum and dad have gone...they are not forgotten...so they will never truly die anyway."

Yew stood looking at the shocked faces of the crowd as tears rolled freely down her face and dripped off her chin. She noticed several others were in tears from her words, then she remembered they were all looking at her and she blushed again.

"Well said." Her Gran was the first to speak even if her voice was shaky from emotion..

The villagers quickly and noisily agreed, they burst into cheers and loud applause. Suddenly Elder Daisy was by her side, hugging her close.

"Very well said." She said in her great niece's ear.

Daisy held her hand up in the air for silence, it quickly fell. "Yew has just encompassed the entire meaning of Samhain for us and has learned a very valuable life lesson. I really couldn't have put it better myself. Let us close this ritual and feast with our Ancestors for they have heard this wonderful young ladies' words for themselves."

Another cheer went up and Elder Bear began reciting the closing words.

Yew wiped away her tears and hugged Blossom and Daisy again. She felt better inside, lighter almost and happier. Indeed, she felt happier than she had for a long time.

"I've learned so much this month that I think October will be my favourite month from now on." Yew smiled a deep, heart happy smile at her family.

Plum the Cautious Witch

An Introduction to Plum

Each of the children of Brew has been named after items in Nature and Plum is no exception.

Named after the Plum tree, which is closely related to its sister, the Blackthorn, Plum has many traits of her namesake. Plum trees are also known as a Faerie tree of dark omen, strong in protective magic. Plum is a fruit wood, and so bears powers of fertility but thorns on the Wild Plum evoke powers of great reserve and protection, the setting of boundaries, and the ability to dissolve them. The wood itself is harder than Apple but has a similar creamy colour, and the branches are tough and knotty. Thus Plum is a wood for the creative artist or anyone desiring to focus on magic that will enhance skill, overcome barriers, keep people or disturbance at bay, evoke toughness and persistence, patience, protection, and healing, especially of the blood.

Our tale begins a month before a Blue Moon. A Blue Moon is a second full moon, which appears every 2.7 years. They are great for adding power to desired goals, heightening spiritual awareness and ceremoniously letting go of something, shedding unwanted habits for example.

Plum is twelve years old, has shoulder length deep auburn hair, which has natural red and deep purple highlights. She is of medium height, well built and rather shy, sadly these lovely attributes have resulted in her being bullied at school.

Plum the Cautious Witch

Plum looked down at her watch waiting for the seconds tick by.

It was taking forever, she decided, as she looked up at the clock on the classroom wall. It showed the same time as her watch. Plum sighed unhappily and tried to read the book before her but the words just wouldn't sink in. Her mind just kept saying over and over; 'fifteen more minutes, fifteen more minutes'.

As each of those minutes ticked slowly by, Plum tried to plan her escape. There were several ways to go and each were good in there own way, but every one of them was also dangerous. When the class bell decided to finally ring, it would mean home time and the end of the school year, then the start of Plum's favourite part, the summer holiday. However, she had to survive the next hour before she could truly relax and enjoy it. Plum ignored her book and stared out of the dirty school window, looking past the sports field and out towards the big grey city beyond. She shuddered, it felt like the tall buildings of the city were glaring down at her like angry bullies. She forced her mind back to her escape and tried to choose her way home.

Plum's mind was so lost in possible escape routes, she didn't see the clock hand had, finally, moved to the right number and she jumped when the shrill bell went off signalling her freedom. After all that thinking, she'd decided to use the library escape route, she hadn't used it for a while and more importantly, Macy and her gang would never be seen dead in the library. Far too geeky for them.

Plum waited until the classroom had emptied and slowly made for the door, ignoring her teacher who was tidying up the text books, she quickly headed out into the hall, checking around her in all directions and instead of going right, towards the front doors of the school like everyone else had, she went left and walked towards the back of the building to the library.

It was empty, of course, this being the last day of term and all the other students were making a bid for freedom. As she walked through the book shelves, a sense of peace enveloped her as it always did in a library. She pretended to be searching for a book but in reality she was heading towards the back of the room to the store cupboard. With a quick look behind her, Plum snook into the small room and closed the door quietly.

She paused for a moment, listening. No one seemed to have followed her and she had escaped the eye of the librarian. Plum took a deep breath, the smell of old books and dust filled her nostrils, she glanced round the boxes of damaged text books, old shelving units and cleaning equipment. She walked to the back of the room and began to climb up the rack of shelving until she could reach the old wooden shutter at the top. With a small creak, she pulled the shutter open to reveal the window. It was just big enough for her to climb through and led out to a narrow ledge and a fire exit staircase.

Unlatching the window, Plum climbed through pulling the shutter closed behind her. Once out, she pushed the window closed, when she heard the small satisfying click, she knew it had closed properly behind her and no one would ever know she had used it to leave the building.

With a relieved breath, Plum walked along the two foot wide ledge to the stairs and carefully climbed down to the ground. For a moment, she stood and listened, there was hardly any noise coming from the front of the school, it seemed everyone had left already. Not surprising really, who hangs around at the end of term? Steadying her nerves, Plum began to walk towards the end of the building hoping to make it round the back of the school, through the fence and into car park of the grocery store next door.

"Going somewhere, Fruit Head?" Macy whinny nasal voice said.

Plum came to an abrupt standstill, her stomach dropped into her shoes and she began to shake.

She had not escaped after all.

Turning, she saw Macy and her gang of girls standing around the side of the building as if they'd been waiting for her. Macy's greasy lank hair hung limp around her skinny angular face as she lent on the wall with a triumphantly smug expression on her face. The rest of her followers were not much better, all of them were dirty and scruffy like no one looked after them. They all enjoyed picking on the loners in the school, like ravens pecking on carrion.

"W...what do you want, Macy?" Plum's voice came out is a weak tremble, her mouth had dried up and her heart beat was pounding in her head.

"What do I want? Well, for starters I'll take that new hoody you've got around your waist." Macy pushed herself away from the wall with her foot and took several steps towards Plum.

"No, it was a birthday present." Plum said bravely.

"Did Fruit Head just say no to me?" Macy said and glanced around at her gang with a sickeningly evil smile on her face. They all nodded and laugh excitedly like stupid hyenas.

Plum's brain was working too fast, it was trying to work out if she could run for it and get to the janitor's office in the main building before they could catch her. She knew if she could get to Mr. Oliver he would help her, he'd done it before when Macy had pushed her in a puddle and threatened to hit her.

"There's nowhere to run to this time, Fruit Head." Macy said. "You're surrounded."

Plum glanced around her and saw Macy was right, the gang had surrounded her. Her heart pounded more loudly in her chest as if trying to escape and her breath came quickly now as she realised she was trapped and in serious trouble.

"My name is Plum." She said as she stared at Macy, her fear making her tremble. Her brain wondered why she was making this worse but she chose to ignore it.

"Your name is Fruit Head." Macy said as her friends giggled. "Now give me that hoody."

"No."

Macy took the last two steps towards her and stood just inches away, she glared down into Plum's face, "What did you say?"

"I said, no." Plum shouted. All the fear and anger of being bullied by Macy and her gang for the last year, boiled to the surface and exploded in an uncontrollable rage.

For a few seconds Macy was stunned and looked at her uncomprehendingly. Then, without warning, Macy's right fist flew through the air and hit Plum on her left cheek. It happened so fast that Plum was on the ground and in agony before she knew what had happened. Macy's friends cheered and laughed as the pain throbbed in Plum's face making her want to vomit. She lay as still as she could, her hand holding her bruised face.

Macy leaned over her, untied the hoody and roughly pulled it off Plum's body. "See, it gets you nowhere to say no." She grinned maliciously. "Hmmm...I think I will take your backpack too, I need a new one for next year." She grabbed the bag, shook out all of Plum's things onto the dirt and began to walk away with her friends. Before they turned the corner, however, Macy turned around and said, "See you next year, Fruit Head."

Plum could hear their laughter and cheering as she lay on the ground with her eyes shut trying hard not to cry. 'You should have just given her the stuff, stupid.' Her brain said. She let the tears come as she tried to sit up, she was still wobbly but at least she had stopped feeling sick. Finally, she got back up on her feet and angrily brushed off the tears. She dusted off the dry soil on her uniform and noticed a grass stain on her shoulder.

"Great." She said to herself, now she would have to explain it to her mum and she knew it would not make her mum happy. She picked up her pencil case, lunch box, old note books and headed for home. With each step nearer home, Plum could feel herself getting happier and happier, the knowledge of not seeing Macy and her friends again until September, which felt like months away even though it was only six weeks, was a very happy feeling indeed. It was such as good thought that she was smiling by the time she reached her front door and unlocked it.

Plum always got home an hour before her mum, it was their agreement that Plum would wash the breakfast plates and cups and then start her homework. However, today was different as it was the end of term she had no homework, sadly she also had no hoody or backpack. Plum tried to push all these thoughts from her mind and went to get changed out of her uniform. Looking at the grass stain on her shirt and sighing, she hid it in the washing basket by putting other clothes over it hoping her mum wouldn't see it.

After doing her chores, Plum grabbed her favourite book and went upstairs to read in her bedroom until her parents came home.

"Plum? Dinner's ready, can you set the table, please?" Asked mum.

"Okay." Plum called downstairs.

By the time Plum had sorted the table, her mum was bringing the food through and placing it on the tablemats. Peri, Plum's mum, was a small olive skinned woman who always looked like a gypsy in the romantic stories with long flowing skirts, embroidered loose tops, long dark hair and colourful jewellery. Plum sometimes wished she was more like her mum but she knew she was adopted as a baby and had no idea what her real parents looked like.

"This looks great, love." Said Rue, Plum's dad. A tall man with strawberry blond hair and freckles.

Peri smiled at her husband as they all sat down to have dinner together.

"How was school today, Plum?" Rue said.

"Same as usual." This time, instead of forcing a smile, which was her usual facial expression, she was truly happy for the end of term.

"Looks like you are happy it's over for the summer though." He winked at her.

Neither of her parents knew about Macy and how she hated Plum, she had decided not to tell them when the bullying first started because if she told and Macy got in trouble because of her, then the bullying would be far, far worse. So Plum had kept it to herself for the whole year, telling no one.

"We have some good news, Plum." Mum said.

Plum looked up from cutting her food.

"Your father got the teaching position he wanted, the one we talked about, do you remember?"

"Umm...yeah. Which one was it again?" Plum tried really hard to remember which one but her dad had talked a lot about different jobs over the last few months.

"The one at Brew Elementary School, the school in the country, the one you said you liked the sound of." Dad said.

"Oh, cool. Well done, dad." Plum said and smiled at him.

Her dad's face glowed with pleasure. "Thanks, love."

"Will it take you much longer to get to work now?" Plum said.

"No, actually, it won't." Dad said and looked at mum.

"Plum, how would you feel about moving to the country for your dad's new job? I know how hard it can be to move away from your friends." Mum said.

Plum held her fork half way to her mouth and looked startled, "Move? We would move to the country? Forever? Really?"

"Well perhaps not forever, love, but yes, we would move to the country. Your dad's job, the Headmaster job, comes with a cottage on the school land. So we already have a house to live in. Will you be terribly sad to leave here?" Mum asked looking worried.

"Sad? No. I'm very, very happy to move. This is awesome!" Plum said as she leapt from her chair and rushed over to her dad giving him a big hug and then to her mum doing the same before sitting back down again. "Tell me everything about the new place, I want to know everything." She said with a big smile on her face and a truly happy heart.

Mum passed dad the bread rolls and said, "Well, I guess we worried about that one too much."

"I guess so." Rue said and laughed. He then began to describe the village of Brew, the new job and new school they would both be attending.

Over the following weeks, Plum's family prepared for the move and began packing. Thankfully, Plum's mum had not found the grass stain on her shirt as she was far too busy rushing around sorting and packing to notice it.

Plum's father was not expected at the school until the start of the new term but they would be arriving in Brew two weeks before then to settle in and start to feel at home. The house they were now in was rented and their landlord wished them well in the country and their new lives.

As their car pulled into the drive of the Headmaster cottage, Plum let out a breath that she hadn't realised she had been holding. True freedom at last, she thought. She would never have to put up with Macy and her gang bullying her again. A new calm and sense of peace blossomed inside her, something she had not felt for a long time. By the time she got out of the car and got her first proper look at her new home there was a smile firmly fastened on her face.

The cottage was built of stone and stood on a wooded plot. At the front there was a small flower garden with a bird bath and a sun dial, at the side there was a garage and round the back there was a kitchen garden and small lawn. Everything was surrounded with trees. The cottage itself was single story, however, it had a window in the roof and Plum hoped the attic would be her bedroom.

Plum's parents had hired a van, which her father had driven down from the city while her mum and Plum had come in their car. None of them began to unpack and they all stood looking at the cottage.

"Oh, it's lovely, Rue." Mum said as she hugged him happily.

"Yes, it is. Shall we go and take a look round before we do anything else, ladies?" He said.

"Yes." They both replied.

Plum loved it, the cottage seemed bigger on the inside than on the outside. There were three bedrooms, one of which her father would use as a home office, a large kitchen, a living room and two bathrooms. As it turned out, two of the bedrooms were upstairs in the attic with a small bathroom. Plum's room was upstairs as she had hoped and she saw that her window looked out over the back garden and the trees.

"Do the people here know we're Pagan, mum?" Plum asked as they sat at the kitchen table eating lunch amongst boxes and bubble wrap.

"Oh yes, love. Everyone who lives in Brew is Pagan, so we no longer have to keep our religion quiet, we can openly attend rituals. Would you like that?" Mum said.

"Yes. This place is so awesome, I love it already." Plum said.

Mum and dad looked happily at each other and dad squeezed mum's hand.

"I understand from the email I got from the Elders here that there is a Blue Moon Celebration for the ladies next weekend." Dad said.

"Really? Oh, that will be fun and a great opportunity to meet everyone." Mum said. "Do you want to come with me, Plum?"

"Sure." Plum said absentmindedly as she tried the chop up the pickled onion on her plate and gave up popping it in her mouth whole.

After lunch, Plum continued to help her parents to unpack and while she did so, deep dread began to build in her stomach, what if there was another Macy here, here in Brew, in her new school or even at the Blue Moon Celebration. The very thought made Plum want to run and hide. How could she avoid telling her parents this time seeing as her dad was to be the Headmaster of her new school? Panic gripped Plum and she accidentally dropped the vase she had just unwrapped, it hit the tiled kitchen floor with a loud crash and shattered into a hundred pieces.

"You okay?" Mum said as she rushed back into the kitchen from the lounge.

"Yeah, fine. Sorry, it slipped out of my hands." Plum said as she grabbed the broom and began to sweep up.

"It was just an old vase, it doesn't matter as long as you are okay. Did you cut yourself?"

"No." Plum said. "Mum?"

"Yes, love?"

"Do we have to go the Blue Moon thing?" Plum didn't look her mum in the eye, she just swept up the bits of pottery and placed them in the bin.

"We don't have to but I think we should, it would be a good way to meet our neighbours and perhaps some of the girls at the new school."

"I guess."

"Don't worry about it, if it's not enjoyable we shall come home early, how's that?" Mum said as she gave Plum a quick hug and headed back to the lounge.

"Okay." Plum called after her.

"Oh, Plum? When you've finished that box, can you go down the lane to the grocery store and fetch some milk and bread, please?" Mum said as she popped her head back around the kitchen door.

"Yup."

"Thanks, love. Ask your dad for some money, I think he's still unloading in the garage."

By the time Plum walked down the lane to the shops, it was mid afternoon on a warm August day. There were flowers growing at the bottom of the hedges that lined the narrow country lane, lots of different ones that Plum didn't recognise. She looked around and could just see the school buildings over the high hedges to the right. The birds were singing and the sky was bright blue with just a few fluffy clouds floating by on the warm breeze. Plum sighed with happiness, she decided she much preferred the country to the grey, dirty city.

Plum walked for the first time into the centre of the village and was delighted by what she saw. The village of Brew is gently placed around a central village green and around that green sat the local shops, which included the bakers, the butchers, a general store and a post office. Each of the stores were originally houses and fitted in nicely with the other old houses and cottages of Brew. Although there were a few other stores around the village, down side roads and lane, none of them were like the shops found in the city. None were overly modern and horribly commercial with plastic or neon. The village had managed to maintain it's old fashioned feel.

Plum walked around the green until she came to the bakery, a wonderful scent of warm freshly baked bread filled her nose as she entered the shop. Inside was an amazing collection of shaped loafs, buns and even cakes. Some were in the shape of the moon, ready for the celebration, others were sun shaped and some were even in the shape of a bundles of wheat.

After purchasing the bread from the nice woman behind the counter, Plum headed towards the general store for the milk. Although, the store was small it was packed with goods, in fact it was difficult to see any spare shelving space because they sold so much. Plum noticed that many of the items in the store were made by locals and had Brew addresses on the labels. After having a good look round, Plum bought the milk and headed for the exit and just as she reached the door, it swung open and a group of talking and laughing girls walked in.

Plum froze instantly, expecting to be called names like she had been at her old school every time she saw Macy and her friends. In her panic, she rushed past them, bumping into them accidentally.

"Hey!" The girl with the short, spiky blond hair said.

"Careful!" The girl with skin the colour of chocolate called out as she stumbled against the newspaper stand.

Plum ignored them in her fear and quickly walked out the door that one of them had held open for her, without even saying 'thank you'.

"You're welcome." The girl with long dark hair, who had held the door open, said a little sarcastically.

Horrified that she had found another Macy and friends here in Brew, Plum raced home. She dumped the bread and milk on the counter in the kitchen and raced upstairs to her bedroom. Luckily neither her mum nor dad had seen her return so she was able to take a few minutes to try to calm herself. Although, she was still shaking, Plum managed to put the fake smile back on her face and go downstairs again.

"I thought that was you, love. In a hurry for the bathroom, were you?" Dad said jokingly as he walked in from the garage.

"Yeah, too much OJ, I guess." Plum said, glad her dad had unknowingly given her an excuse to run upstairs. "Here's your change." Plum emptied her pocket onto the kitchen table and went to put the milk in the fridge.

"Thanks, love." He scooped it up and put it into his pocket. "What did you think to the village? Did you find the shops okay?" He said as he switched on the kettle.

"Yes, it was easy. The other end of the lane takes you right to the village green and the shops are all around it."

"Ah...I thought that was it, sounds nice. I can't wait to have a look around. Did you meet any locals?" He said.

"Yeah, a few." Plum said and avoided his eye.

"And?"

"And what?" She said as she looked out of the kitchen window pretending to be distracted.

"Ah, there you are." Mum said as she entered the kitchen carrying a big empty box. "Did you find the shops okay?"

"Yeah. Do you need a hand?" Plum said, hoping to change the subject.

"Sure, can you break down this box and add it to the pile in the garage, there's also another empty one in the lounge. Thanks, love." Mum said as she passed the box to Plum and sat heavily on a kitchen chair.

Plum was glad for the unexpected opportunity to escape the conversation with her dad and took the empty boxes out to the garage. When she returned to the house she could hear her mum and dad talking to someone in the lounge. She headed towards the voices as curiosity got the better of her.

"Oh, that's lovely. How very kind of you." She heard her mum say as Plum walked into the room, stopped dead in her tracks and gasped.

The girls from the store were in her lounge, talking to her parents. Plum's heart sank as she stood in the doorway and could only stare in horror.

Everyone had heard Plum's gasp and they all turned to see her shocked expression. Plum could see the girls recognised her and saw they were shocked too.

"Ah, there you are, Plum. I was just saying 'thank you' to these lovely young ladies who brought over dinner for us to-night as a welcome gift from their families. Isn't that kind?" Mum said and smiled encouragingly.

Plum nodded, speechless and glared at the girls.

"This is Plum our daughter, who is normally more chatty but seems she has lost her manners today." Her father said giving a warning look to Plum.

"Hello, Plum. It's nice to meet you." Said the one with the short, spiky hair. "I'm Yew and this is, Holly, Hazel and Ash."

"Hello." The other girls said in unison.

"Hi." Plum said warily watching the girls.

"Well then, like I said, this is very kind of your families. Please do say thank to them for us." Dad said.

"We will." Said Holly, the one with long dark hair.

Plum's mum was just seeing them out the front door when the Ash, the blond haired girl asked if they would see her at the Blue Moon Celebration on Friday night.

"Oh, yes. Plum and I are looking forward to it." Mum said.

The girls all looked at Plum and then back at her mum.

"See you on Friday then girls." Plum's mum said as she closed the door behind them. She walked back into the lounge and picked up the large stew pot, "Can you both bring the other food in the kitchen, please." She said to Plum and her dad.

They all placed the food on the table. There was a huge stew, homemade herb bread, a bottle of wine and a big chocolate cake.

"What was that all about, Plum?" Dad said, "You weren't very nice to those girls and they were only being kind."

"I...I" Plum searched her brain quickly for a suitable answer, "I didn't know what to say, I don't know them."

"Well, a thank you would have been a good way to start." He said.

"I know, I'm sorry." Plum blushed, she was ashamed of her rude behaviour.

"Perhaps you can say thank you and sorry when you see them on Friday night." Mum said. "You need to make friends here and those girls seemed very nice."

"Hmm...." Plum said, not convinced.

The next few days blurred into one long unpacking, cleaning and organizing effort with the whole family pitching in. On the Thursday, while mum was painting the kitchen walls a nice warm yellow colour, Plum finished stacking all the boxes in the garage, ready for recycling.

"There you are." Dad said as he came in the garage side door.

"Yup. Just finished tying these up into bundles for the recycling collection, mum said they are due in the morning." Plum said.

"Thanks, love. You've been a great help with the move." He said and smiled at her. "I have to take my office stuff over to the school before it starts again next week, do you want to come with me and see your new school?"

"Yeah, it will be nice to see it." Plum said while trying desperately not to show the dread that was building inside her at the thought of the start of term.

"I'm just going to get my key from one of the town's Elders, Elder Heather is my deputy and teaches Herbology. You will like her, she is a nice lady. I meet her when I came for the interview. Oh and you might want to clean up, you have black marks on your face, love." Dad said with a chuckle.

"Do I? Okay, I've finished my jobs so I was going for a shower anyway. Do I still have time for one?"

"Oh yes. I'll let you know when I'm back and ready to go."

The Brew Elementary School stood a little back from the road and was set in several acres of gardens and playing fields. Built with rust coloured red bricks, the building looked a lot more interesting than the one made of steel and glass that Plum had attended in the city. The eight stone steps at the front led up to the wooden doors of the main entrance.

Plum noticed that all the windows were clean, the gardens were neatly kept and there was no litter anywhere in sight. "Looks nice, dad." She said.

"It is nice, love. Wait until you see inside." He said as he walked up the steps and unlocked the main doors. He quickly disarmed the alarm and wedged the front door open before heading into the hall.

Plum looked at the open door, "Why are we leaving the door open?"

"Elder Heather and a group of students are bringing in some new compost for the greenhouses while we're here, ready for the start of the new term."

"Oh, okay." Plum said as she stepped through the doorway and stood with her mouth open startled by the view.

The hallway, which was half lined with wooden panels below art posters and event flyers, lead down past several doorways to huge glass doors. The doors stretched from floor to ceiling and beyond them was an enormous round room surrounded by glass with a blue ceiling. Oddly, within it stood a large Oak tree around which sat wooden seating. Plum walked quickly down the hallway to try to make sense of what she saw. She soon realised that it wasn't a room at all but a huge, round, open courtyard and the blue ceiling was actually the sky.

Rue, Plum's father was waiting for her at the large glass doors with a huge smile on his face. "Amazing, isn't it?"

"Yeah."

"Come and have a look in the courtyard." He said as he opened the glass door.

Plum walked out onto one of the four paths leading towards the tree, there were several wooden benches under the tree and on the grassy areas between the paths. She stood and looked around.

"The school is built like a wheel, it's central area is this courtyard." He said, "There are four parts of the main school building and each section is dedicated to an element, so the North section is Earth, East is Air, South is Fire and West is Water. Each of the sections join together here in this courtyard.

"Wow." Plum said.

"I thought you might like it. What is even more interesting is how they have arranged the outbuildings. The swimming pool is the building adjoining the West section, the green houses are accessed through the North section, the main Physical Education department is the other side of the East section and the art department with the pottery kiln and blacksmith shop is through the South section. Clever how they put the subjects and element together, huh?"

"What a cool school."

"Yes, it is. Let's get the boxes from the car and put them in my office, then you can have a look round while I unpack." He said.

"Okay." Plum already liked the school, she just wasn't so sure she would like the students so much. From what she had seen they looked just like the bullies from her last school. Trying not to think about Macy again, Plum helped her dad to get settled in his new office. While emptying the car she'd noticed there were two other cars in the car park, although she couldn't see anyone else around.

Leaving her dad to unpack, Plum went for a wander around the school. She looked through the windows of the doors to the classrooms and found that they all had wooden panelling on the lower half of the walls while on the upper halves were wooden cupboards or shelves or pictures. The classrooms were so different to what she was used to that she began to imagine herself sat in each class enjoying the school work. A rare thought indeed.

She checked out the pool and although the door was locked, she could see it was a big pool with diving boards. She then made her way down the next hallway that led out to the art department buildings. This external door was locked but she could see the art buildings were like the main one and built in red brick. She then headed towards the North section and the greenhouses, she had put this one off until last knowing there would be people there. The door out towards the two big glass greenhouse was unlocked and standing slightly ajar. She could hear people talking but couldn't see them.

"Mind out of the way, please."

A voice came from behind Plum, she spun round to find two groups of students, carrying heavy bags of home grown compost, walking straight towards her. She leapt out of the way just as the first group reached her and struggled through the doorway out towards the greenhouse.

"Hello, you must be Plum, Rue's daughter. It's nice to meet you. He said he was bringing you along to see the school today." Said the tall thin lady with long grey hair that was fastened up in a bun on her head.

Plum stood holding the door for the other group of students, "Yes, hello." She said shyly.

"Good, good. I'm Elder Heather, your father's deputy and teacher of Herbology. Do you think you can be a dear and hold that door open a bit longer? There's one more group of students coming from my car with bags of compost, I got a really good batch of compost going at my house this summer and thought I would spread the goodness around the greenhouses." She said, her face lighting up with enthusiasm.

"Okay." Plum smiled, she liked Elder Heather already.

"Thank you, Plum. Once the other students have come past, you can come and help if you like, the more the merrier." Elder Heather said with a big smile that lit up her face and she set off towards the massive greenhouses.

Plum watched her and the students disappear from sight and heard another group approach from behind. Turning round again she held the door open for them, only to realise that two of the four students carrying bags were the same girls from the shop and from her lounge the other day. Plum began to blush at her rudeness that day but as she did, she began to feel angry. Angry at herself for blushing and angry at the girls for being here when she was having a good day and ruining it.

As they got to the door, Plum turned round and walked out letting the heavy door close behind her with a loud bang. There was no way she was hanging around to be bullied again, she decided. As she walked away, she heard a shout and looked back towards the door, there was spilt compost everywhere and one of the girls was crying. Plum was rooted to the spot.

"Hey, what did you do that for?" The other girl shouted at her angrily as one of the students ran to find Elder Heather.

"I didn't do anything." Plum said.

The girl with long dark hair stalked towards her, "You did, you saw us coming and shut the door on purpose. You trapped Ash's fingers in the door." She said.

"I didn't do that." Plum said getting angrier by the minute.

"You let it go without even checking and walked away." The girl said.

Determined not to be bullied again at this school, Plum lost control of her temper and shoved the girl, "Stay away from me and don't go telling people I did that or you will be in big trouble." Plum shouted.

The girl looked stunned and speechless. Plum felt a sheer pleasure of knowing she was in control for a change and would now be deciding who would be in trouble and who would not. She glared menacingly at the girl.

"Holly, what happened?" Elder Heather said as she came rushing from the greenhouse.

The girl, Holly, replied, "Ash's trapped her fingers in the door." With one last look at Plum she took Elder Heather over to the Ash who was now sat on the ground holding her fingers and crying.

Plum plunged her hands into her jeans pockets and enjoyed her new found power, she would no longer be pushed around, told what to do or called names by other students. A happy glow grew inside her as she made her way back to her dad's office. She didn't tell him about Ash's fingers nor Holly, she decided she didn't care about them, just as they wouldn't care if she had hurt herself.

"You seem in a good mood, love. I guess you enjoyed your wander around the school. It's has a nice feeling about it, doesn't it?" Her dad said as they pulled up into their drive a few minutes later, having only taken the car because of the boxes.

"I am, I think I am going to enjoy going to school next week." Plum said with a smile, knowing she would never be bullied again.

That night Plum had terrible nightmares about big plants with legs escaping the greenhouse and eating all the nasty children, it had saved her for last. The nightmare woke her up and she sat in bed with her light on for a long time, waiting for her eyelids to feel heavy again so she could snuggle down and go back to sleep.

The following day, Friday, Plum felt tired and her eyes felt gritty from lack of sleep. She began to think about the Blue Moon Celebration that night, only instead of there being a sense of dread, she now felt excitement and looked forward to it.

The night had turned chilly as Plum and her mum walked with the other women of the village down a side lane towards the Goddess Mound. The mound was a steeply sided hill in the shape of a pregnant stomach where all celebration rituals were held by the villagers of Brew. Tonight was a Moon ritual for the Blue Moon, exclusively held for the women of the village. The grassy path leading up to the top of the mound was lit by flaming torches as the women gathered and began their ascent to the top.

As Plum and her mum, Peri, came around the last turn of the path they could see the entirety of the top of the mound. Thirteen standing stones formed a circle, each one lit with a torch. As was usual in the Moon rituals, the women were allowed to stand within the circle of stones and made a ring around the central stone altar and fire pit, the fire within the pit burned brightly and lit everyone's faces with golden light. In the centre, next to the altar, stood Elder Heather and another lady.

"Elder Heather and Elder Daisy are the leaders of the women's rituals here in Brew." Mum whispered to Plum.

Plum nodded her understanding and looked around the circle at the women's faces, some she had met at the village when fetching shopping, and others she didn't know. Some, however, stood out as if a light shone over their heads showing them in the darkness, these, of course, were the girls. Plum looked at them all and looked away, trying not to care what they thought of her as they all stared in her direction.

"Hail and welcome ladies to a very special Blue Moon Celebration." Elder Heather said.

"Hail." The women of the village replied.

"As we know the phases of the Moon are very special to women as it coincides with our body's changes but a Blue Moon is a rarity in itself."

Elder Daisy stepped forward, a small woman with shoulder length curly grey hair and a happy face, "Firstly, I would like to welcome two new ladies to our circle, Peri and Plum." She said holding out her hand towards Plum and her mum in presentation.

The ladies of the circle cheered as Peri and Plum smiled and nodded thanks.

"A very happy day indeed when we can welcome new friends to our village." Elder Heather said. "A Blue Moon is an excellent time for fulfillment and manifestation, a time to gather what we've sown and to take responsibility for our actions. It is about endings and a powerful time to release, cast out and unburden yourself. You can take this time to step out of an old skin, identity, behaviour or attitude."

Plum's mind wandered as she thought about Elder Heather's words while the ritual continued on around her. There was something to the words that struck a cord in Plum's mind, a truth she could feel in them, even if she could quite grasp it at present.

As the ritual moved on, Plum saw Elder Daisy move around the circle handing out something but she couldn't see what it was.

"Elder Daisy is coming round with pieces of wood and charcoal pencils. I want you to write a word or a short sentence on it that represents what you wish to let go of, anything you have been holding onto for the last year but can now let go of. Then each of you can speak a few words about it, if you want and we shall burn the wood."

There was a low rumble of conversation as the wood and charcoal pencils were passed around. Some ladies stood or sat on the ground, other, more aged ladies, sat in their folding chairs to contemplate what they wanted to remove from their lives and write on their piece of wood.

"Remember ladies, it can be anything from a bad habit to a negative emotion, from a toxic relationship to an old emotional scar. Whatever it is that you no longer want in your life, now is the time to burn it away and as we burn our wood we release the words and everything connected with it, into the universe and cleanse it from our being." Elder Daisy said as she finished giving out the pieces of wood and pencils.

Plum had no idea what to write, she glanced at her mum who looked like she was thinking deeply. She looked around her at all the women who were in various stages of thought or writing. At last, her eyes fell upon the girls and she spotted Ash with her bandaged fingers struggling to write her word with her left hand and a look of sheer concentration on her face. When she stopped writing, Ash's face showed relief and pride that she had managed, despite her injury.

Plum recognised that emotion on Ash's face, she'd seen it on her own face whenever she had managed to get home safe and avoid Macy and her gang. A frown appeared on Plum's forehead and the cold fingers of guilt began to grow in her stomach.

Peri glanced at her daughter who was now deeply frowning, seemingly lost in her own world and had not written anything on her wood.

"Having trouble thinking of something, love?" Mum asked.

"Actually, no, I've just thought of one, thanks." Plum said as she wrote it down and stood waiting for the others to finish.

"Alright ladies, if you've all finished collecting your thoughts." Elder Heather said. "We're now going to arrange ourselves around the fire for the remainder of this ritual. If you would please gather your chairs." Elder Daisy said.

Within a very short time, all the ladies were seated around the large fire, in a circle. Plum was sat next her mum and another Elder by the name of Poppy. Plum had been introduced to the women who were Elders before the ritual at the meeting place on the Village green. She had liked Elder Poppy, even if she was one of the girl's mothers, Rowan's mum to be precise. Elder Poppy was kind and friendly to Plum right from the start.

"As we celebrate this special Blue Moon we are also celebrating the end of things, things that have held us back or have become useless in our lives as we grow and move forward." Elder Heather said.

"This is a circle of trust, everything that is said here will stay here, it is considered confidential and is a bond between all who sit with us under the Blessed Moon." Elder Daisy said as she looked up to see the perfect full moon in the cloudless sky.

Elder Heather stood holding a piece of wood in her hands. "I will go first. I have written on my wood the word Jess. Jess was my most beloved cat and the eldest of all my cats, who died at the beginning of the year, as most of you know. She was the first cat I got when I moved here many years ago and has been with me through all the good and bad time's, always offering cuddles. I miss her terribly but I now know I can let her go and remember her in my heart. I will stop comparing my other cats to her and appreciate them for their own personalities." She said as she got closer to the fire, "Hail Jess." She said as she threw the wood onto the flames.

"Hail Jess." The ladies said in unison.

"I have written one word on mine too." An old lady's voice came from across the circle. She remained seated in her chair, a cane lay across her lap. "I have written the word fear. For many years I have been afraid for my Granddaughter Yew."

Plum noticed that everyone turned to look at the group of girls, one of them blushed and looked at the old lady.

"As you know, I have looked after Yew since her parents died and I recently had a scare of my own when I broke my hip. I know I've been over protective of Yew, afraid something would happen to her or me. I think you will all agree she has lost enough. Since my accident, Yew has shown me how brave and strong she can be and how much better life is when we share it rather than hiding behind fear. Hail Yew." She said and threw her wood into the fire.

"Hail Yew." The women said with one voice.

As the women continued to present their words or thoughts to the circle and burn their wood to the chorus of hails from the other women, Plum stared down at her word, her brain racing nervously for her turn although with excitement and not dread as was her usual feeling when she was about to be the centre of attention.

There was a prolonged silence as everyone waited for the next person to have the courage to stand and speak.

Plum jumped to her feet and felt everyone's eyes on her.

"I...I'm..." She began nervously, "I'm Plum...I'm new here, we just moved here...I mean my mum and dad and I just moved to Brew." She took a deep breath and tried to slow down her wildly beating heart.

Mum reached out her hand and touched Plum's encouragingly.

"I want to say sorry to Ash for her hand. Yes, I was holding the door and I walked away. I didn't realise her hand was there or I would never have it let go. I'm sorry Ash, it was an accident." Plum looked over towards Ash who nodded at her and smiled.

"I want to tell you all about my old school and some people there. Some girls...well...Macy and her friends used to push me around, steal my things, call me names and tear up my homework."

"Why didn't you tell us?" Mum stood up quickly.

"I didn't want you to make it worse." Plum said.

"Oh, love." Mum hugged her tightly.

Silence fell on the audience.

After a few moments, Elder Poppy broke the silence, "Plum, please try to carry on with what you wanted to say."

Peri sat back down looking terribly worried but allowing Plum to continue.

"Anyway...I was so happy when I found out we were moving away from the city and I wouldn't have to see them again. Then I met some of the girls here and I know I panicked, so it didn't go well. I was afraid they would be like the Macy and I ran past them, pushing them out of the way. I decided I was not going to be the one being picked on this time and thought that if I could be in control, it would stop anyone who tried to be horrible to me." Plum said, as tears welled up in her eyes and tumbled down her hot cheeks.

"I now know I was wrong and I'm sorry for how I acted. I know I was becoming like Macy and although I liked it at first, I now feel bad and guilty about it. I'm sorry that I took it out on you all." Plum looked directly at the girls, "I know it was wrong of me. I understand now that you have tried to be nice and I pushed you away because I was scared." She looked down at her piece of wood and took another deep breath, "My word is Bully. I want to forget about Macy and how she made me feel and I don't want to be like her." Plum threw her wood into the flames, returned to her seat and burst into sobs as her mum lent over and hugged her again.

"Hail Plum." Elder Heather said.

"Hail Plum." The ladies answered and cheered her for her bravery and honesty.

Plum wiped away her tears, she felt better inside for having let out everything she was feeling. Her mum continued to hold her hand as they sat and respectfully listened to the others speak.

"Everything will be okay, love. But you must tell your dad and I everything that happened, will you do that?" Mum whispered in Plum's ear.

Plum nodded and her mum squeezed her hand encouragingly.

The rest of the ritual was a blur to Plum as her mind and heart reeled from telling everyone the truth. Even she was amazed she had stood up and done it. Elders Heather and Daisy brought the ritual to a close and announced it was time for the feast. A table was set up and all the potluck dishes the ladies had brought were set out and everyone began to help themselves.

"Plum?" A voice said behind her.

"Yes?" She turned around to find Elder Heather stood behind her.

"You were very brave, Plum. Well done." She said with a big smile.

"Thank you." Plum said and blushed.

"Not only did you show courage and honesty but I think you also learnt that the basic meaning of Honour is respect and means treating other people the way you want to be treated. It's a commitment to live by standards that earn you respect from others. More importantly, if you live that way, you can honour and respect yourself and never be ashamed of what you've done. Yes, very well done." She said as she smiled, nodded approvingly and walked away to get food.

"I'm very proud of you, Plum although you should have told us everything when it was happening, I'm so glad you worked out the right and wrong of it and so bravely apologized. You are growing up to be a good person, love." Mum said.

"Thank you, mum." Plum said as she hugged her mum again, feeling happier than she had in a very long time.

"Excuse me."

Another voice came from behind Plum. She turned round and was surprised to see all the girls stood before her. Plum's pulse began to race and her mouth went dry with a familiar fear but this time she stood her ground.

"I think we should start again. My name is Ash and these are my friends, we hear you are new and would like to welcome you to Brew." Ash said with a big smile on her face.

Yew stepped forward before Plum could speak, "Hello, I'm Yew. It's nice to meet you and welcome to Brew."

As Plum began to open her mouth to say something, the other girls all said 'Welcome to Brew' and a huge smile spread across Plum's face. She found herself utterly without words.

"Hi, I'm Holly." Said the girl with the long dark hair and the welcoming smile, "I just wanted to say...welcome home."

Glossary of Character Names & Meanings

Amber (F) Fossilized tree resin (not sap), which has been appreciated for its colour and natural beauty since Neolithic times.

April (F) The fourth month in our modern calendar.

Ash (F) A medium to large tree, which grows in most parts of the world.

Aster (F) Popular garden plants because of their attractive and colourful flowers.

Bay (M) A bay is a large body of water connected to an ocean or sea formed by an inlet of land due to the surrounding land blocking some waves and often reducing winds.[1] Bays also exist in in-land environments as an inlet to any larger body of water, such as a lake or pond, or the estuary of a river.

Bear (M) Large mammals. Although there are only eight living species of bear, they are widespread, appearing in a wide variety of habitats throughout the Northern Hemisphere and partially in the Southern Hemisphere. Bears are found in the continents of North America, South America, Europe, and Asia.

Birch (F) A medium to large tree, which is only usually found in the northern hemisphere.

Blossom (F) In botany, blossom is a term given to the flowers of stone fruit trees and of some other plants with a similar appearance that flower profusely for a period of time in spring.

Brook (M) A small stream.

Buck (M) Male antelopes, deer and goats are referred to as bucks (larger species of male deer such as elk or moose are called bulls). Male hares, rabbits, ferrets, rats and kangaroos may also be referred to as bucks.

Calder (M) A river in Scotland.

Camellia (F) A flowering plant found naturally in eastern and southern Asia, from the Himalayas east to Japan and Indonesia.

Cherry (F) A fruit tree, its fruit is also called a cherry.

Daisy (F) A common flower in the same plant family as the Aster and the Sunflower.

Drake (M) A male duck, also a term used to describe (particular types of) dragon. A Drake (fairy) is a type of fairy found across Germanic and Northern European Folklore.

Fern (F) A very old plant, which has stems, leaves, and roots but reproduce via spores and have neither seeds nor flowers.

Finch (M) Seed-eating songbirds with many sub-species that can be found around the world.

Fleur (F) French for flower.

Flower (F) A flower of a plant, sometimes known as a bloom or blossom,

Furze (M) A thorny evergreen shrub with beautiful yellow flowers, very common upon the plains and hills of Great Britain; called also gorse.

Hana (F) Means flower in Japanese.

Hazel (F) A temperate shrub or small tree with broad leaves, bearing prominent male catkins in spring and round hard-shelled edible nuts in autumn.

Heath (M) A heath or heathland is a shrubland habitat found mainly on low quality acidic soils, and is characterized by open, low growing woody vegetation.

Heather (F) The heather family is a group of flowering plants found most commonly in acid and infertile growing conditions.

Holly (F) A widely distributed shrub, typically having prickly dark green leaves, small white flowers, and red berries. There are several deciduous species of holly but the evergreen hollies are more typical and familiar.

Honey (F) A sweet food made by bees using nectar from flowers.

Ivy (F) A species of evergreen climbing or ground-creeping woody plants native to western, central and southern Europe, Macaronesia, north-western Africa and across central-southern Asia east to Japan and Taiwan.

Juniper (F) Junipers vary in size and shape from tall trees to columnar or low spreading shrubs with long trailing branches. They are evergreen with needle-like leaves.

Lily (F) Flowering plants growing from bulbs, all with large, prominent flowers.

Marsh (M) A type of wetland growing grasses, rushes or reeds rather than woody plant species. Marshes can often be found at the edges of lakes and streams

Oak (M) A tree that bears acorns as fruit, and typically has lobed deciduous leaves. Oaks are common in many north temperate forests and are an important source of hard and durable wood used chiefly in construction, furniture, and (formerly) shipbuilding.

Opal (F) A gemstone consisting of hydrated silica, typically semitransparent and showing varying colours against a pale or dark ground.

Pearl (F) A hard, lustrous spherical mass, typically white or bluish-grey, formed within the shell of a pearl oyster or other bivalve mollusc and highly prized as a gem.

Peri (F) Short for Periwinkle. An old world plant with flat, five-petalled flowers and glossy leaves. Some kinds are grown as ornamentals, and some for use in medicine.

Poppy (F) An herbaceous plant with showy flowers, milky sap, and rounded seed capsules. Also grown for medical uses.

Rain (M) Moisture condensed from the atmosphere that falls visibly in separate drops.

Rock (M) The solid mineral material forming part of the surface of the earth and other similar planets, exposed on the surface or underlying the soil or oceans.

Rose (F) A prickly bush or shrub that typically bears red, pink, yellow, or white fragrant flowers, native to north temperate regions.

Rowan (F) A medium to large tree, which grows in most parts of the world. Also known as the Mountain Ash.

Ruby (F) A precious stone, colour varieties varying from deep crimson or purple to pale rose.

Rue (M) A perennial evergreen shrub with bitter strong-scented lobed leaves that are used in herbal medicine.

Saffron (F) An orange-yellow flavouring, food colouring, and dye made from the dried stigmas of a crocus.

Sage (M) An aromatic plant with greyish-green leaves that are used as a culinary herb, native to southern Europe and the Mediterranean.

Seal (M) A fish-eating aquatic mammal with a streamlined body and feet developed as flippers, returning to land to breed or rest.

Stone (M) The hard, solid, non-metallic mineral matter of which rock is made, used as a building material.

Tamarack (M) A slender North American larch, a bird of the larch family.

Thorn (M) A stiff, sharp-pointed, straight or curved woody projection on the stem or other part of a plant.

Timber (M) Wood prepared for use in building and carpentry.

Violet (F) A herbaceous plant of temperate regions, typically having purple, blue, or white five-petalled flowers, one of which forms a landing pad for pollinating insects.

Willow (F) A tree or shrub of temperate climates that typically has narrow leaves, bears catkins, and grows near water. Its pliant branches yield osiers for basketry, and its wood has various uses.

Wolf (M) A wild carnivorous mammal that is the largest member of the dog family, living and hunting in packs. It is native to both Eurasia and North America, but has been widely exterminated.

Yew (F) A coniferous tree that has red berrylike fruits, and most parts of which are highly poisonous. Yews are linked with folklore and superstition and can live to a great age; the timber is used in cabinet making and (formerly) to make longbows.

More Titles from Edain Duguay

Chameleon
   (YA fiction, paperback & eBook)
   Published by Wyrdwood Publications 2013

Pagans on the Wildside: Campfire Cooking
   (Recipe collection, eBook)
   Published by Wyrdwood Publications 2009

Pagan Poetry for the Seasons and the Festivals
   (Poetry collection, eBook)
   Published by Wyrdwood Publications 2008

About
Wyrdwood Publications

Wyrdwood Publications is a small eco-friendly publishing house, founded in 2006, which specializes in Pagan and Heathen eBooks.

As an independent eBook publisher, based solely on the Internet, we have a responsible 'green attitude' to the publishing of our eBooks.

For EVERY 'Green Leaves' eBook we sell, a tree will be planted!

This book is a 'Green Leaves' book and you have helped a tree to be planted in a deforested area of the world.

Go to our Green Leaves Policy page on our website, for more details on how we are incorporating green ideas into our publications business and helping to make a difference to the environment we live in.

www.wyrdwoodpublicatios.com

CPSIA information can be obtained at www.ICGtesting.com
Printed in the USA
LVOW06s0400060314

376034LV00008B/32/P

9 780987 998088

CPSIA information can be obtained at www.ICGtesting.com
Printed in the USA
LVOW06s0400060314

376034LV00008B/32/P